Mukoma's Marriage and Other Stories

Emmanuel Sigauke

Booklove Publishers

BOOKLOVE PUBLISHERS
P O Box 1917, Gweru, Zimbabwe
E-mail: booklove87@yahoo.com

Mukoma's Marriage and Other Stories

First published 2014

Editor: E A Makadho
Artwork: Paul Chirodza
Cover Design: Gigasoft   InDesign

ISBN   978 0 7974 5660 0

Published in Zimbabwe
by Booklove Publishers
printed by Serveplus Investments
2014

Mukoma's Marriage

Mukoma[1] got married the year I turned seven. He had returned from South Africa three months before, and had brought a stylish record player, which caused many young women in Mhototi to flock to our home. They danced and paraded before him, waiting to be chosen. And he chose Alice, the youngest and prettiest of them. Shortly after, Alice frequented our home, until, during the month our mother visited her sister in Chivi, she started to spend nights in Mukoma's bedroom hut. During the day, she would station herself in our kitchen hut, cooking and singing, while Mukoma sat in the bedroom, listening to the radio or playing some South African records, and he occasionally joined her to talk, sing and laugh. He even helped her cook, something I had never seen him do before. I wouldn't ever have suspected that he knew how to cook. He smiled a lot too, often inviting me to join them in the kitchen. I fell in love with Alice's food and showed up whenever she was cooking. She would give me pieces of meat to taste, asking, "What do you think Fati? Good *handiti*?[2] And I would say yes, the meat, or fish, or chicken, yes, was good.

One Sunday afternoon, I entered the kitchen and found Mukoma showing Alice how to fry eggs. She was listening and watching carefully as he explained the process. "You have to make sure the cooking oil is not too hot before you put the eggs in." Mukoma lifted the frying pan. "Make sure the oil is hot enough, but not so hot that it produces smoke." They laughed, he the loudest, she shyly. "Of course, you would never do that, would you?" She didn't say anything, and kept her eyes down. "Overheat the cooking oil?" he said, his voice softer. She shook her head and leaned back to laugh some more. Mukoma put the pan back

---

1   Mukoma - elder brother
2   *handiti?* - isn't that so?

on the fire, and broke an egg directly into it. The egg slid to the centre of the pan and hissed in the cooking oil; then it moaned as the oil danced around it. It smelt nice, and I started to chew the inner layer of my lips.

"Perfect," Mukoma said. "You don't want to burn this beautiful face," he touched Alice's face, "this little moon of mine." Her face was light-complexioned and shiny.

Alice chuckled and said, "I know. My sister damaged her face while frying eggs. You know the scar on her chin?" She suddenly had a morose look on her face. Mukoma rubbed her shoulders, raised her face with his open palm and with a radiant smile looked into her eyes. She lit up again and said, "Since then I have learned to be careful when frying. I want to make sure I keep your moon beautiful."

Mukoma nodded and lowered his face close to hers. I looked away.

I left them cooking and went outside, but Mukoma called me back and said, "Hey, I want you to run to the stores and buy a loaf." He looked at Alice and said, "Or maybe two? What do you think?"

"One is a lot," she said, smiling.

"Ok, get two loaves," Mukoma said. "You don't have to run today; you can play on the way."

He handed me some money and I almost wanted to thank him, not for the money, but because he had said I could play on the way. I was gone for a while and returned only with one loaf, the last loaf left in the store. Although I played alone, kicking my ball all the way to Vhazhure and back, it didn't seem like I was gone for a long time.

They were done cooking when I arrived, and they looked calm, as if cooking made them calm. They were not singing anymore, nor were they talking much, but Alice maintained a weak smile as she dished out the food. We ate what Mukoma called a rich breakfast of eggs, liver, bread, and two items I didn't know. Through all this, I watched what Alice was doing, how she seemed to know where our mother's pots and plates were as if she had always lived with us. And how she made

Mukoma smile, while she remembered to smile too, which in turn made me smile. We looked like a family.

For lunch, Alice prepared a big pot of *sadza*,[3] beef stew, fish, and fried chicken. Everywhere I looked there was food, and for a moment I didn't know if I was going to have an appetite to eat more, but I was not one to let food go to waste.

"If you're tired of *sadza*, there is rice too," Alice said, showing me a large black metal pot. She hadn't used mother's clay pots in all her cooking so far, preferring the steel ones Mukoma had brought from South Africa. The kitchen had that smell Mother always called "Jeri's smells of Joni." My nose twitched and my mouth watered. Alice had cooked so much food that I didn't think any more cooking would be necessary for a whole year.

"I'll have rice, yes," I said, "and chicken."

Alice fixed me a plate and as I sat down to eat, Mukoma entered the hut and went straight to a plate of *sadza* and fish which Alice had already prepared for him, but she had not made a plate for herself. They both ate from Mukoma's plate, feeding each other, and glancing in my direction every now and then. When they kissed, I pretended not to have seen them. Enjoying my food, I didn't mind them showing how happy they were together. I knew if they were happy I would be happy too.

After lunch, they went to the bedroom hut, leaving me gnawing on a chicken bone. I would have the remainder of the day to myself, with no one paying attention to what I did, so I started tasting the fish and the beef. The bream was really good. The beef was too salty for my liking, but it was still good enough to earn Alice my praise. Although I didn't get a chance to tell her that her food was good, I knew Mukoma would tell her for me.

---

3   *sadza* - very thick porridge made from maize meal or rapoko or millet, etc

When I got tired of eating, I decided to take a walk to Chisiya, one of the hills that flanked our home, to look for my sometimes-friend, Chari, who never came to my home to ask me to play; he just went straight to the hill and waited there, hoping that I would show up. As was to be expected, I found him leaning against a rock, aiming a catapult at a huge *mutsviri*[4] tree nearby. I tiptoed forward so I wouldn't startle his bird before he shot it, but I soon noticed that the catapult was empty. Poor Chari, if only he had thought of coming to look for me at home, he would have feasted too. But his mother, like mine, didn't allow him to eat in people's homes.

"Your mouth is shiny," he said when he saw me. "What did your new *maiguru*[5] cook for you this time?"

"What *maiguru* are you talking about?" I said, wiping my mouth with the back of my hand, which I then wiped clean on my T-shirt.

"Don't pretend you don't know who I'm talking about." He pointed at our home with his pouted mouth. "I saw them together, climbing into your brother's lair." He always called our bedroom a 'lair', and I was proud to be part of the lair, but I had no time to talk about it right now.

"Let's go play in the Gonera cave," I said, already thinking about provoking the honeybees in there.

Chari's eyes lit up and he started skipping about, singing "*Baya wabaya!*"[6] as if he expected the swarm to attack us. I didn't join in the singing. I was too full to sing.

We climbed to the top of the hill and entered the cave which housed the most famous beehive in the whole village. We really were not supposed to be there, but Chari said he wanted the bees to attack the village. "There's just too much evil in this village," he said, panting from his hopping from rock to rock as if he was a *ngururu* or mountain goat.

---

4 *mutsviri* - a Zimbabwean indigenous tree with hard wood
5 *maiguru* - elder brother's wife or his girlfriend
6 *baya wabaya!* - prod you prodded! (a song of victory, meaning it's a done deal)

"What evil are you talking about?" I asked, hoping he didn't think Alice spending time with Mukoma was evil. I certainly didn't think it was, wouldn't even consider it so. Besides, Mukoma wouldn't have cared what Chari or anyone thought; he did what he wanted, whenever he wanted to do it.

"There's just too much nonsense going on every day here, the war and everything," he said, sounding serious, as if he knew what he was talking about. Then he burst out laughing and hopped onto the next rock, by the entrance of the cave. I jumped too and nearly pushed him off the edge of the rock, but he balanced by grabbing my arm. I did not agree with him on his talk of evil, and there was really nothing he or I could do about the war that was going on. I did not care whether the bees attacked the village or not; I just wanted to provoke them, to see what they would do to us.

"You're the face of evil!" I said to Chari, but he ignored me and gave me his back. "*Muthakathi!*"[7] I added. This made him laugh, most likely because he didn't know what the word meant. Mukoma had told me it was a Zulu word from a war chant. That's all I knew. The word sounded good. I was even certain that the comrades used the word when they attacked the soldiers. But I didn't care about the war. Mukoma did not care about it too since it had arrived in our village when he was in South Africa. It was not his war, he used to tell me, and no one could make him join the comrades. He didn't even allow Alice to call herself a *chimbwido*[8] like most village girls who got excited when the comrades were in the village.

Chari and I started stamping the dusty floor of the cave. What we liked most were the echoes the cave produced whenever we stomped and shouted. Eventually, that's what would anger the bees, and they would send a messenger to check the area out. We would flail our arms

---

7   *Muthakathi!* - a Ndebele term for a witch or wizard
8   *chimbwido* - a female war collaborator who assisted the guerrillas in the Zimbabwean war of liberation

at the messenger bee to send a clear message of war back to the hive, and when it left, we would prepare to escape. That was the plan which had succeeded only once before, when we had brought Tavonga here. We had planned it — we wanted him to be strong, to see how fast he could escape an angry swarm. Initially, we were going to escape together, but that's not what ended up happening. Chari and I managed to run away without receiving a single sting, but the bees had caught up with Tavonga and stung him until he passed out. He recovered from all the swelling in two days, but told us he would never go back to the cave again. And, of course, even Chari and I were not supposed to come back here, but we had decided that nothing would stop us, ever.

The bees didn't come again this time, even after we threw little rocks at the darker end of the cave, where their hive was located. The ways of these bees were mysterious. They were called *gonera*[9] because this was their permanent home, and some said they were sacred, connected to our ancestors. The elders respected them, and before they sent men to harvest the honey once a year, they did some rituals to ask the ancestors to pacify the bees. Sometimes they acted furious, the bees did. Once they attacked Tukano who had tried to get some honey without following the proper procedures. They pursued him from the top of the hill to his home. They entered every hole and crack, attacking his wife, children, dogs and cats, chasing the whole family to the river. The family dove into a pond and stayed under water. The bees formed a thick layer on the water, waiting for them to come out. I don't remember how that had ended, but it was a story much talked about in the village.

Since the bees didn't seem interested in stinging us, Chari and I left the cave and went to slide down the smooth rock facing our home. Chari didn't want to slide; he just kept looking at our home and shaking his head. "He's a lucky man," he said. "I wish I was his age."

"Why do you say that?"

---

9   *gonera* — bees connected to the ancestors

"Didn't you leave them there?" he asked. "And they are still there inside."
He was pointing at Mukoma's bedroom hut. "Don't expect them to come
out soon. They're there doing this." He was thrusting his thumb between
two fingers. He started chuckling; then suddenly, he slid down the rock, lost
his balance on landing, and fell on his stomach. When he sprang up he was
still laughing. And he started twisting his waist as if dancing to *kwasa-kwasa*[10]
music.

"They will be out by the time I return home," I said. "Alice has to go back
to her home."

"And to think that she's way younger than him," he said, shaking his
head.

"How do you know?" I asked.

"Because I'm older than you, fool..." He looked at the bedroom hut
again. "Everyone in Mhototi Village knows. Some say she's only fifteen.
Isn't your brother like forty?"

"No, he told me he's eighteen years older than me."

He squinted at the sky, chewed his lower lip rapidly, then said, "So that
makes him what, let's see," the squint narrowed further, followed by another
rapid chewing of the lower lip, "that makes him…twenty-six." He widened
his eyes and looked at my home again. "He's almost like her grandfather!"
He gave a brief laugh, like a cough. "But they say it doesn't matter though.
Once a woman has these, she's ripe." He cupped his hands on his chest to
suggest breasts. I ignored him and slid down the rock again, landing neatly.

To me, Alice looked like a big woman, and she was the right height for
Mukoma. I know she was the right age for him too. She had a good smile
and knew how to cook. Chari didn't know what he was talking about.

At sunset, I went back home and found Alice in the kitchen, cooking
again. After greeting her I proceeded to my brother's bedroom where I

---

10   *kwasa-kwasa* — a dance rhyme from the Democratic Republic of the Congo that
        started in the 1970s. In the dance, the hips move back and forth while the hands
        move to follow the hips.

found him flipping through one of the magazines he had brought from South Africa, the ones he always told me not to touch, even though I so wanted to touch them, especially after Chari had told me I better touch them. But I would not dare touch them, because Mukoma had promised me a thrashing if I ever did; and the last thing I wanted on this earth was to let any part of my body come in contact with his massive fists that had demolished Simango, the village drunk. Simango was never quite the same after that fight at Vhazhure Centre, a fight which had not really been a fight because no sooner had it started than Mukoma hammered him on the forehead, sending him flying into a nearby thorn bush. I couldn't touch his magazines; let him look at his magazines alone.

After I had settled on a small stool in the room, Mukoma closed his magazine and looked at me. His eyes were tired little pits, but roving still, as if they were suspicious of something I would or wouldn't do. I lowered mine, which accidentally landed on the magazine, I quickly shifted them from there and returned them to him and they were held in place.

"Tonight you sleep in the kitchen," he said. "We have a special guest." He paused and pursed his lips, one side forming into a smile, the other maintaining a curl of seriousness. Then the lips dropped fashionably, something that I associated with his having spent too much time in South Africa. "Of course, you know her — you spent the day with her."

I knew her, and I would be glad to sleep in the kitchen.

"Make sure you don't wet Mai's[11] mat. If you do, I will..." He formed his hand into a fist. "Do I even need to tell you what will happen?"

"No," I said. "I'll not wet the mat."

"Good. You're a big man now."

"I'm very big, yes." I nodded and smiled.

---

11   Mai — Mother

8

"Now go and sit with your *maiguru* in the kitchen. Tell her I'm coming soon."

I found Alice eating a piece of fish, which she tried to hide when she heard me entering the hut, but then resumed eating when she saw it was only me. She gave me a small piece too, and as I chewed I watched her cook, thinking of what Chari had told me. We sat in silence as if she had nothing to talk to me about. When she was done, she fixed me a plate of *sadza* and fish; and then another, which she took to the bedroom hut. Again, I ate freely, wishing that moments like this would last forever.

That night Alice slept in Mukoma's bedroom. I didn't miss the lair at all. I slept soundly in the kitchen. No dreams of running away from goblins, or of flying over rivers and mountains to places I didn't know. I had dreams of swimming with fish, of feasting on Alice's food. In those dreams, Alice cooked more mountains of meat, left frequently to join Mukoma in the bedroom, came back to cook more food. I woke up after the sun had already risen.

Outside, I saw Mukoma walking into the compound, returning from somewhere; maybe he had walked Alice to her home, or he was returning from the river since he liked to bathe early in the morning when the water was still cold. Walking towards the bedroom hut, he smiled at me and, as he started climbing into the house, he turned his head and said, "Don't try to get in here. I need to rest a little." He then disappeared into the bedroom before I had a chance to say anything.

I walked back towards the kitchen, but before I reached the door, I heard a squeal of metal behind me and turned to look. My heart beat faster when I saw Alice's brother, Misheki, opening our small gate, and behind him, Alice walked slowly, her arms folded across her chest as if she felt cold. Shirtless, Misheki looked angry, his hairy chest heaving up and down, as he tore across our compound to Mukoma's bedroom. He carried an axe on his bare shoulder, a knobkerrie in his left hand, and what looked like a spear in his right. People didn't just walk around with spears unless they were going to an ancestral gathering, but Misheki

9

was certainly not going to anything resembling an ancestral gathering. I didn't like the way he advanced to our bedroom, and I knew Mukoma wouldn't be very pleased either upon seeing Misheki walking like that into our compound.

They walked by me like I was not there, and when they reached Mukoma's door, Misheki leaned his knobkerrie and spear against his thighs and held the axe steady with both hands, as if he was about to hack into the door. I wanted to pick up something, a rock or stick, and throw it on the roof to awaken Mukoma, but I found nothing. Misheki tilted his head to Alice, and then nodded violently. Alice tiptoed forward and tapped on the door.

"Knock harder!" Misheki said.

Alice did as commanded, but only after coughing out a brief laugh, as if the whole thing was wasting her time. She knocked again, louder than before, and Misheki moved forward, pushing her out of the way. He raised his axe higher.

The door swung open and Mukoma's face, deformed by sleep, appeared first, level with the axe's blade; then his whole body heaved into view, shirtless too, but his chest was not hairy. His face stretched with surprise and when he lowered his look towards Alice, he relaxed and flashed a smile, which was followed by a frown. I moved closer to the scene.

"Can I help you?" asked Mukoma in a voice I had never heard him use: soft, low, even sweet.

"You know this young woman?" asked Misheki, authoritatively, poising his axe.

"Easy with that thing," said Mukoma, pushing the axe away gently.

"Do you know her or not?" asked Misheki, shaking with anger.

Mukoma didn't answer. His eyes scanned his surroundings again, first shifting from Misheki back to Alice, and then to me. When they resettled on Misheki, they dulled. "You found out about us, didn't you?" He said this with more ease than the situation required. But if you knew

Mukoma, you wouldn't have been surprised. I was afraid of what might happen if Misheki didn't get out of the way.

Misheki dashed closer to Mukoma, who backed and raised his hands as if in surrender.

"Do you know her?" Misheki asked.

Mukoma nodded, but I wasn't sure if he was agreeing. Misheki put the axe down and grabbed the spear and knobkerrie. I didn't want to see a fight, not another one. Only two weeks before, Mukoma had thrashed Mai Linda's[12] new husband at a beer gathering, and I didn't like how people talked about that fight. Mukoma had not told me about it, which meant that even he thought he had gone too far, had crossed the boundaries of fighting, as he once told me. But with the way Misheki was acting, shaking his knobkerrie and spear in Mukoma's face, in front of the man's girlfriend, oh no, things could turn ugly easily.

Alice started to walk away, but her brother grabbed her arm and said, "You stand as close to this man as possible. I want him to take a good look at you and declare he knows you. Otherwise someone dies today."

Mukoma laughed. Misheki stiffened and made as if he was about to enter the house to murder someone. Mukoma reached behind the door and revealed a spear. He then descended the two stairs of his hut with the spear positioned to clear the way ahead of him. Then when the spear was about to pierce into Misheki's stomach, Mukoma stopped. He sighed and looked at his weapon as if in admiration. The spear was one of the items that he had told me not to touch, and the only time I had seen him brandishing it was when he was possessed; they said his spirit was of a former Shangani warrior and hunter from Mozambique. People said his spirit, like other restless spirits, enjoyed taking the living for a ride. So brother became a Shangani warrior and hunter when he got possessed. The one time I had seen him possessed, long before he

---

12   Mai Linda — Mother of Linda

left the country for South Africa, he had swung this very spear as he leapt into the air and chased animals no one could see. But he never talked about his spirit; in fact, he once told me he didn't want it known that he got possessed sometimes.

Misheki backed up too, but raised his spear higher and shouted, "I'm about to damage you, Jeri."

"Just know that you may be damaged back too," said Mukoma, shaking with laughter.

"Do we need to go through this?" Misheki said. "Do you really want to tempt me to harm you?" He then grabbed Alice by the arm and pulled her so that she was made to stand, shivering still, silent, between the two men. "Here is your wife, and like a good *mukuwasha*,[13] welcome me in your home properly— accept your responsibility."

Mukoma pondered. I drew closer.

Alice looked at Mukoma with eyes full of questions; then she said, "Please tell him if you know me." Then she turned to Misheki and said, "Could you move back a little so that some of us can breathe?"

Misheki moved back as requested, so far back that he stopped by my side.

"I want to hear you say in your own words that you have something to do with her not showing up when we were expecting her last night," Misheki said, his voice softer.

Mukoma, my guardian, the only man in the village who wore a suit, stretched and straightened, looking first at me, then at Alice, and said, "That's the first thing you should have said. Not your little show here."

Misheki gripped his spear more firmly and advanced. Mukoma stumbled backward and raised his arms again in surrender. "Okay now, let's not get too excited." He then looked at Alice with a smile. "Of course, I know her."

---

13   *mukuwasha* — brother-in-law (in this case, sister's lover or sister's husband)

"And what are you going to do with all that knowing?" said Misheki.

"Now I see what this is about," said Mukoma, who then turned to me and said, "Do you see what they are trying to do here, little man?"

I shook my head, but ended up nodding. He smiled at me and said, "You're not helping." Then looking at Alice, he said, "Of course, my wife can stay here, if that's the reason you brought her back."

At that point, Misheki gathered his weapons and started walking away, hitting the ground hard with his brown boots. But before he had covered much distance, he stopped, turned to look at the couple and, pointing at my brother with his spear, said, "We'll give you one week." He resumed walking, but stopped again. "Only after you pay up, like a real man should do, will we be able to welcome you in our family. But if you take longer than a week, someone is going to be harmed."

"Give me two days," Mukoma shouted at Misheki's back. But Misheki kept walking as if he had not heard him. Mukoma then took his wife into his bedroom and closed the door. At that moment, as the door finally fastened, I realised that I would not share that bedroom with Mukoma ever again, and I started smiling; in fact, I wanted to laugh out loud, but people would think I was crazy.

When Misheki reached the edge of our compound, he stopped walking and turned. He stood looking at the closed bedroom door for a while, then shook his head, pointed at me with his spear and walked away. I soon remembered that before the arrival of Misheki and Mukoma's wife, I had been trying to open the kitchen door to choose some food for breakfast.

Pocket Money

I started school in 1977, the year Mukoma sneaked out of the country and went back to South Africa. One night before he left, he came to my bedroom hut to show me my new school books. Those books smelt sweet and looked delicious. Sitting on my reed-mat bed, I smiled, picturing myself at school mingling with other pupils from villages like Gudo, Mudhomori, Magwidi and Magetsi. I couldn't wait for the night to be over.

Mukoma flashed a smile and said, "These are not sweets, but love them the way you love sweets." He paused and after a moment of chewing his lips, added, "Love them more than sweets." Casting his glance from me to the books and back, he smiled, the first time I had seen him smile in a long, long time. I smiled too, imagining that school was a world of smiles.

The incident reminded me of an earlier one, the first time he had given me my own packet of sweets. He had never before given any child in the extended family a whole packet. He surprised me when, behind his bedroom hut, he handed me the sealed packet and said, "All yours." Although drunk, he did not stagger nor stumble over his words. "Eat as much of them as you want, when you are done, share with others what's left." He had grinned — his first grin in a long time — and looked at the packet in my hand, then at my face, and nodded. "Sounds great, right?"

I didn't answer, couldn't think of words to say, but everything he said sounded great.

"You don't have to share them with the other kids," he said. "They're all yours, from your true brother." He lit a nice-smelling cigarette, and through clouds of smoke, watched me fish out favourite pieces. "Maybe you can give away the ugly ones," he said, sucking his teeth and coughing out a brief laugh.

"I'll eat them all," I said. "They're all my favourites."

"You do what you want," he said, pulling at his cigarette, his eyes looking away from me.

Mukoma had always brought me sweets from when I was two and still living with my grandmother in Mafuva. That was when no one knew who would claim me, and I didn't know what was going on, didn't even think about what I was supposed to know. But I liked it when he used to come to Mafuva. The sight of him—a tall, dark man with handfuls of sweets—always brought smiles on my face. He came to Mafuva in a grey shirt with white stripes and blue jeans. I lived with my grandmother who had taken me in after my mother died. People said my mother died a month after giving birth to me. But I didn't think a lot about her because once I met Mukoma, he told me he would take me to Mother. He said it like a song; he said it loud and sweet: "One day, when I'm ready, I'll take you to a place where there is Mother." He told me that he was visiting me from a faraway place, this place he would take me to one day. When he told me about this place, I would smile and laugh and ask him questions I don't remember now, and the air around us would be warm, the sun shining only for us. He would sit with me outside Grandmother's hut for a short time, and never went inside. Later, I would be told that the people in my grandmother's village were our enemies, and I would find out Mukoma never went inside her hut for that reason. But I never found out why and how they were enemies. Could it have been that they were witches, my grandmother's people?

Years later, after I had already gone to this far place, after I had already turned eighteen or nineteen, I discovered that Mukoma was the first son of my father, who had declared from the very day I was born that he would raise me, despite the fact that I was the child of a woman who had stolen his father from his mother. He had come to take me on that long bus ride that sent trees flying in the opposite direction, and

15

the next thing I was one of many children growing up together in the Mukaro family of Mhototi, a family and a village that would always remind me that I had come from somewhere, which I knew, and that my only true relative was Mukoma, which he was proud of, always telling me, "We are only two; two sons of a man who came from Mozambique and never returned." Always, I would nod, even when I didn't understand what he was telling me, and he never failed to give me sweets.

Content at last, as if my fishing through the packet of sweets was a skill he had expected, Mukoma had patted me on the shoulders and walked back to where other men sat drinking beer. I stayed behind the hut until I had eaten the best sweets. I decided not to give away even the ugly pieces. Mukoma's favour that night had meant a lot to me, but I had not felt as special as I did on the night he showed me the books, the night before I started school at Mhototi Primary.

Mukoma's wife, Maiguru MaMoyo,[1] had already told me that I would borrow Ranga's used books since he was two grades ahead of me. Ranga, the son of our neighbour, always got the books he wanted. His uncle, who had inherited Ranga's mother when her husband died, worked in Zvishavane when it was still called Shabani, and he bought all the books for Ranga. He always said young people should be allowed to learn. "Who knows," he would say, "when this war ends, they may become our leaders and take our village out of its poverty." Since Ranga had all the books needed at school, and some extra ones to read for leisure, many parents came to borrow the ones he no longer needed.

Maiguru had told me to respect Ranga so he would consider giving me his Grade One books. That's how it had always been; she too had borrowed her first school books from pupils in upper grades. Well, I didn't have to depend on Ranga now, so I didn't have to respect him. Other pupils would come to me to borrow my books too when I went into the upper grades, but I wasn't going to give the books away. I

---

1   Maiguru MaMoyo — elder brother's wife MaMoyo (she is of Moyo totem. Moyo means heart)

would keep them piling until I ran out of space. Then I would build myself a house of books, and I would read them whenever I wanted.

And Mukoma was saying, "I present to you these books as your torch into the darkness of ignorance." Then he coughed out a laugh, just as he had done the day he handed me the packet of sweets. "They are your swords, they are your guns." I had no idea what he was talking about now, but if books were swords, if they were guns, I liked them more.

Yet I sat there trying to understand him, my Mukoma, man of big words. But then I decided not to understand him and to focus on those books instead. I sat smiling, looking at the light as it reflected off the shiny covers.

Years later, I would try to understand what he had meant, but that was to no avail. He had been clear that night about his aspirations for me though: "I want you to tighten your belt and walk into this jungle of life where, with these torches, you will live a life even happier than mine."

I could not imagine ever growing up to live a happier life than his, the way he smoked his cigarettes and emitted smoke with curled lips; the way everyone talked about all the money he had. The way they always talked about him as "Our Man from Joni."

"This is the road I wanted to walk but I never was able to," he said, pointing at the books. "Now I want you to walk it well, go places that I may never be able to see." Father had died while Mukoma was still in Standard Four, and there had been no one to pay for his school fees. "But you don't worry about me," Mukoma said. "I'm the one who worries."

"I'll go everywhere," I said, but I didn't know what I was talking about. I liked that my words made him laugh though. Throughout my school life, I would always think about how my love for books made him smile, and about how I had promised him that I would explore the world.

Mukoma lit a cigarette and smoked while I looked at the pictures in the new books. There was some magic in them, something about their smell of newness, the brightness and smoothness of their covers. I would flip a page to see the next picture, try to read the words, but failed, yet those pictures told many stories, and carried many promises about a future of endless learning, which I would grow to call a long friendship with books.

When Mukoma finished smoking he sent me to the kitchen hut to fetch him a cup of water. He wanted to teach me how to read, so he sat with me on the mat. I was surprised because I had never seen him read a book before, except the magazines with lots of pictures that he had said I should not touch.

He had bought me three different books. One was for English, a language he said I was going to learn at school, the other was for Shona, which he said was the formal name of the language we spoke, and the third was for what he explained as the numbers subject, Mathematics. As he explained each book, he looked in the air as if he was thinking about something serious; then he would let out a brief laugh, shake his head, and continue, nearly choking on his own words.

I knew what English was because I had heard him speak it with his friends and when Mai said things like *"Fofaksek!"*[2] I knew she was speaking in English. Once in a while, old men and women at beer gatherings would argue, and always ended using English words like *"Brarry furu!,"*[3] "I blast you!" and "You idiot!" Maiguru used some English too, and, once, she told me that I was *"stupet,"*[4] and the word sounded nice coming out of her mouth. Later, I would use that word at school and when the headmaster heard me he told all present that I was learning English fast. He told me that I would grow up to be an expert in English. English was all around me; even the birds sounded English.

---

2   *fofaksek!* — for fuck's sake!
3   *brarry furu!* — 'bloody fool!' (a phonological corruption of the expression)
4   *stupet* — a phonological corruption of the word 'stupid'

As Mukoma showed me the English book, I wished that Maiguru had been there to read it. Mukoma had left her in their bedroom, but I would ask her to read some of the books to me since I knew she knew some English. Mukoma read several words and asked me to identify the corresponding pictures. Then he read some more of the words, all the way to the middle of the book, and when he stopped, he said, "Your turn."

I looked at the book blankly. He stroked my head, laughed and said, "Don't worry; one day you will be teaching people how to read this language." I smiled and focused on the pictures. Mukoma read some more words.

On top of that, he was telling me that even the language we spoke was taught in schools. "If you think you know anything about our language, wait until you start learning it in school. Some people study it at the university." He paused. "But you wouldn't know yet what a university is; I didn't know for a long time too."

He started to read from the Shona book. I was struck by the simplicity of the words and the sentences, and the number of pictures in the book. Mukoma showed me the pictures first and asked me what they were. With the English book he had read the words first, and then showed me the pictures. I tried hard to explain what I saw in the pictures: hens running, cattle grazing, a dog and a cat playing, dogs chasing a hare, a cat catching a snake, a grandmother talking to a grandfather. Some of the pictures were of beautiful homes that no one in Mhototi could ever dream to build.

The Mathematics book was full of colourful shapes and numbers.

"These are detachable," Mukoma said, but I did not understand what he meant. "Once you start school, and when you begin to use this book, the teacher may ask you to remove these shapes from the book so you can use them in groupwork with others." He paused to allow me to admire the book, which I held with shaking hands.

"Good, huh?" he said.

"I like pictures and shapes and words and English and Shona,' I said.

He laughed, then said, "You'll understand one day what you just said. But it's a good sign that you like shapes. People who love these shapes tend to end up with good jobs after they finish school, so never stop loving shapes." He looked towards the door, and with his eyes acquiring a distant look, he mumbled something about wars, then suddenly he smiled and refocused on the books. "Shapes are everywhere." He said these were not all the subjects I would learn in school. "Soon, you'll find out that learning is a ladder with endless steps waiting for you to climb."

Mukoma opened the English book again and read so fluently that I sat there hoping one day I would read as well as he did, the way his voice collapsed and escaped through his nose, his lips curling as if the words were disgusting. He retreated to his normal voice only to explain in Shona what he had just read. The stories were nothing like anything I had ever heard, but I liked to hear more of them. The story that struck me the most was one about an egg-shaped boy who fell and cracked his egg body. Mukoma had a hard time stopping me from laughing at the boy, and I could not wait to tell Chari about this strange little fellow, as my brother called him. He noticed that the strangeness of the images of these people was attracting my attention and he explained, "Sooner or later, you'll know about these. In fact, the war that you hear people talking about will spread to this village too, and you will see people that look like these, *varungu*,[6] the native speakers of English."

"They are the English?" I asked.

"Not all the way, but they are related to the British mostly." He paused, then added, "The only thing I want you to know right now is that mastering their language will get you far."

I didn't laugh as much when Mukoma read the Shona and the Mathematics books. He said soon I would know how to count and spend my own money, once I mastered Mathematics.

"But I don't have money," I said.

---

6   *varungu* — the white people

"I'll leave you some money. We call it pocket money. Not many other children at your school are going to have pocket money. But you have a brother who works where?"

"South Africa-a-a!"

"And how many true brothers do you have in this world?"

"Only one," I said.

"Good boy." He looked at the door as if he was expecting someone to walk in, then he lowered his voice and said, "There will be people telling you lies about how they are your brothers, and telling you this and that; always remember that you have one blood brother on this earth."

He breathed in deeply and lit another cigarette. I wanted him to tell me more about pocket money, so I leaned forward, coming closer to the path of the strings of smoke from his cigarette. I loved the smell of those things.

"You'll have your own pocket money that you shouldn't tell your Maiguru about," he said, looking at the door again. Then he leaned forward and whispered, "It's our secret. Do you know how to keep secrets?"

"Yes, like the secret about the sweets?"

"Right. You'll grow to understand that the life of a man is full of secrets." He paused and started scratching his face. "What other big secret should you keep?"

I scratched my face too, thinking. The packet of sweets was not a secret anymore; I had already talked about it. I knew the books were not a secret; his wife already knew about them.

"You know the big secret, the big-big one that no one in this village should know."

I jerked my head up. "South Africa. I shouldn't tell anyone that you have gone back there."

He nodded and lit his face with another smile, reached in his pocket and brought out some coins. "Here, this is your pocket money."

I took the coins and looked at them long and hard, unsure which shine I liked more, that of the coins, or that of the book full of shapes. Mukoma let me look at the money for a while. "It's all yours." Then he stood up and left the hut.

I had new books and pocket money on my first day of school. I never told Maiguru about the money, which I tied in a piece of cloth and kept for a long time as brother had instructed me. And with that, as with everything else, I became an expert in keeping Mukoma's secrets.

Mupani Whips

Mukoma was the bull of Mhototi, one of the few strong men who had not gone to war. He said he had been lucky because when men of his age were drafted, he had been in South Africa. Now no one could force him to go because he knew how to argue with both words and fists. He said one didn't have to join the guerrillas to be part of the struggle; he was already fighting a great war raising me like his own son. Moreover, he kept healthy livestock, some of which the comrades had as food when they camped in our village.

Mai, our mother, always told me that it would have been better had Mukoma gone to the war. She said he needed to do something worthwhile with his life, instead of entertaining himself with village fights. But I liked to watch Mukoma fight, to witness his massive fists discipline other men as if they were mere boys. Most men who visited our home called him Mukoma, or big brother, instead of Gerald or Jeri, even those older than he. I just didn't like it when he used those fists on me.

When Mukoma was serious about beating me, a beating that would last up to an hour or longer, with short breaks, he didn't use fists; he sent me to fetch a *mupani*[1] whip for myself instead. I often did a good job of fetching the best whip, but on the day I ended up in Mai Ranga's drum, I had it done poorly. The whole thing started unexpectedly, almost playfully, as if it was part of an entertaining dream.

Mukoma had been carving his baboon stools with an adze and smoothing the edges with sandpaper. He had invented these wooden stools that had a baboon carved in the middle of the two flat ends on which people sat. Sitting on them was like sitting on a baboon, and the villagers must have liked doing so because they bought all the stools

---

1 *mupani* — an indeginous tree in Zimbabwe with hard wood and is very straight

Mukoma made. Once, when Mukoma was drunk, I asked him why he made baboon stools instead of other animals and he said that he hated the creatures, notorious maize thieves which not only stole, but also left their waste in our fields.

"And you know their mess looks just like ours," he said, "then their tendency of doing their private business in public; and what's worse, they almost have the same tools that we have." He spoke the last part pointing at his crotch; then he warned me against ever telling Mai that he had told me these grown-up things. I never told her because I liked it when he told me such things, but on the day I ended up in Mai Ranga's drum I swear I could have told her, but she was in Gwenyaya visiting her sister. So Mukoma had no one to stop him from beating me.

The trouble began when I got an adze to make my own animal stool, thinking that I was helping. I knew he would be impressed by my effort since he always told me I shouldn't wait to be told to do things. But I wasn't going to carve a baboon. I drew a picture on the ground to give Mukoma an idea of what I was about to make.

"You can't waste my tree on that." He sighed. "Hares are weak, smart yes, but weak." I sat up, hoping to hear a detailed explanation, but he raised his voice and said, "Carve a baboon!"

I started carving a baboon, and as the head was appearing, the adze missed the wood and sliced some skin off my foot, sending blood squirting everywhere. The sight scared me and I started bawling. Mukoma glared at me and I stopped, but resumed as more blood gushed out. Mukoma's face swelled into a ball of anger, and he threw his adze on the ground and spat.

"Two blunders in one day," he said. "What kind of trouble are you applying for?"

I didn't know what he was talking about, I didn't know what to 'apply' meant, so I kept looking at the blood as it seeped into the soil, but I didn't feel any pain.

"Just tell me this: Are you asking for a sound beating?" he asked, jerking his body forward. I tried to stand, but his stare kept me in position. "First you screw up my shoes, and now this!"

When he mentioned the shoes, I shuddered. He had come close to beating me thoroughly in the morning for placing his shoes facing in opposite directions on the door stoop. He had called me to his bedroom and nearly kicked me in the stomach, but he must have seen something on my face because he restrained his foot and opened his mouth to say something but closed it. He shook his head slowly, and then said, "Don't do something this stupid again."

But now here I was, having just failed to show him that I could be careful. It wasn't the wound that frightened me, nor the blood, but the shame I felt for letting Mukoma down.

I wiped my tears and stood up. The look on Mukoma's face was telling me what to do, so I started limping away, but when I felt his eyes crawling on my legs, I straightened up and walked like a man.

"Don't waste that trip!" he shouted.

I walked faster towards the thicket near Runde River, which was made up mostly of *mupani* trees, to fetch a whip, but I decided to do things differently. Instead of fetching a *mupani* whip, I went to a *mubhondo*[2] tree. I thought *mubhondo* whips were less painful — they looked so. I also thought Mukoma would smile when he saw that I had shown some independent thinking. But boy, was I wrong when I returned and showed it to him! His quick eyes told me I had to fetch the usual *mupani* whip, so I immediately ran back to the forest.

When I returned home, whip in hand, I found Mukoma smoking a cigarette. When he did not look at me immediately, I knew there was no room for forgiveness, so I tiptoed forward, extending my arm to hand him the whip. Soon, the beating would be over, and I would wash my wound with salty water. But something told me to stop walking,

---

2   *mubhondo* — an indeginous tree in Zimbabwe with hard wood

stop handing him the whip. There was a moment of silence, as if in all of Mhototi, in all of the world, there were only two people, Mukoma and I, thinking about a whip.

Mukoma threw the cigarette stub on the ground and stamped on it with his boot; then he looked at me with red eyes, then at the whip. The whip didn't satisfy him, but he was not telling me to try again. He wasn't telling me anything. I looked at his hands, which were already swelling into fists, and at his legs, which were shaking. The last time he had beaten me, those legs had kicked me while I rolled on the ground, had kicked me until they got tired. I didn't want that to happen again.

I tiptoed backward, looked to the right, looked to the left; then I turned and broke into a run. Behind me, the mess of wood and half-carved stools toppled over as Mukoma sprung up. I increased speed, running toward Runde River.

"I'm going to kill you, son of a bitch!" Mukoma said, breathlessly.

The wind got hold of my legs and I flew. Soon, I realised that I wasn't flying, when I glanced back and saw Mukoma panting right behind me, slashing forward like a blade. I meandered to the left, jumped over a thorn bush, climbed up and down an anthill, turned left, then right, and heard a heavy thud. I looked back and saw a miracle: Mukoma rolling on the ground, holding his leg. But soon he was up again. "*Blarry* fool!" he cursed as he resumed the chase, but I sped off and away beyond harm's reach.

I ran for a while without looking back. When I finally turned I didn't see him, so I slowed down, but when I looked in front of me again, there he was, standing by a *muvunga*[3] tree, arms outstretched. He smiled and said, "Hello Fati."

I felt the urge to run into those welcoming arms, to enjoy the embrace while it lasted. I wanted to beg for forgiveness, to tell him that I hadn't meant to be careless twice in one day. I wanted to tell him that I didn't

---

3   *muvunga* — an indeginous tree in Zimbabwe with long white thorns

mean to be careless at all. Maybe he would just give me another warning. But my body surprised me when it reversed, turned sharply and took off towards Chimombe's home. I knew that once Mukoma saw that I had sought refuge in someone's home, he would stop chasing after me, as was the norm in the village. We called it *kupotera*,[4] and it saved a lot of children from beatings. I even smiled at my cleverness in remembering that I could do *kupotera*. However, the strategy could only work if there was someone in the home I was entering. And there was.

Chimombe's wife, Mai Kundai, was cooking when I shot into her kitchen. She gasped, sprang up and gathered her skirt tightly around her legs, but let it go when she saw me. "Don't come in here like that!" she said. "Go play outside! This is not a cave for hide-and-seek. Do you...?" Then she jerked her head backward, her eyes directed to the door behind me. I saw a shadow and my heart started racing. Mai Kundai opened her mouth wider, but words refused to come out. I turned and saw that Mukoma had just stepped in, advancing with raised fists. I wanted to escape again, but he blocked the exit. As he stepped forward to strike me, Mai Kundai planted herself between us.

"Stay out of this, woman," said Mukoma, in a low, choking voice.

"You're in my house, man," Mai Kundai said, tilting her head to one side.

"Your house has my animal."

"Aren't you ashamed, such a grown man, storming in after a child *apotera*?"[5]

"Woman, I'm not your husband," he said, trying to catch me. "Get out of the way before you regret this."

Mai Kundai started shaking. "Let me tell you something, *mukomana*,[6] this is my house, and you see that boiling *sadza* on the fire? I can empty the whole pot on you." She gathered herself up like a bird about to take

---

4   *kupotera* — to take refuge
5   *apotera* — has taken refuge
6   *mukomana* — a Shona term for a young man

off. "Out!" she said, but Mukoma didn't move. Mai Kundai looked at me. "Out now both of you!"

Mukoma pushed Mai Kundai to the side and threw his arm to grab me. But she blocked him again. When she moved, I moved, staying behind her as if I was attached to her body. Mukoma thrust himself forward, but Mai Kundai and I dodged. It was like a dance: *siki, nzve-e, siki, nzve-e.*[7] Then when Mukoma attempted to grab her, Mai Kundai screamed, bringing him to a standstill, but the dry scream ceased immediately, as if Mai Kundai had realised its ineffectiveness. Mukoma went *siki* and we went *nzve-e*. Mai Kundai turned her back to the door, allowing me to reach the exit.

I shot out of the hut and ran towards Chigorira Hill, past Chimombe's donkey pen, past old man Bhunga's graveyard, jumped over graves, past the big rock behind which we relieved ourselves every morning. On and on, I ran until I reached the hill. I could go up the hill and hide in the cave of the *gonera* bees, or climb up the tallest *murumanyama*[8] tree and stay there until Mukoma's anger subsided. But perhaps just the cave of bees, to stir up trouble, to provoke the bees and then take off, let the swarm pursue me as I ran back towards where Mukoma was. But those bees were not things to play with; the tree was a better hiding place.

My chest started to burn; I slowed down, looked back and saw him standing outside the hut, still talking to Mai Kundai. I could tell he wasn't done with me; I could sense it — I had never run away from him like this, had never embarrassed him the way I just had. I wanted to run back and apologise, to assure him that if he gave me a chance to go fetch another whip, I would do a good job this time. Then the beating would be over and I would worry about my wound, treat it before it festered.

---

7   *siki, nzve-e* — these are Shona ideophones used to describe someone dashing to grab or beat someone but the targeted person dodges away from the targeted position to safety

8   *murumanyama* — an indeginous tree in Zimbabwe, used for medicinal purposes

With these thoughts I entered Mai Ranga's compound, where a group of men sat around a log fire, drinking beer and talking loudly. I couldn't decide whether to stop at the edge of the compound or tear across without the men seeing me. On the other side of Mai Ranga's home was a stream in which I could hide.

"Someone, catch that hare!" shouted the man who saw me first.

I stopped in the middle of the yard, already thinking of turning and running back to where I had come from, but Mai Ranga emerged from her hut, saw me and said, "What is it, *muzukuru*?[9] Come tell *mbuya*[10] what's the matter."

"I said catch that hare!" shouted the man, who tried to stand up, but fell right back onto his baboon stool.

"Tukano!" said Mai Ranga. "You say one more word and this is the last time!"

"Last time for what?" Tukano asked.

"Just keep on acting like a fool," Mai Ranga said.

Tukano bent forward and laughed. "When these little ones are naughty, it takes a village..."

"Shut your tin!" said VaChigero, the old man with seven wives, who sat on a leopard stool.

"You shut yours, old man," said Tukano. "Don't let me lose respect for you."

Mai Ranga pulled me closer to the fire, and while she parked me by her side, she pushed Tukano's shoulders. "I don't care about the useless coins you give me for my beer," she said. "Leave now!"

Then another man, Mairosi, a friend of Mukoma's, said, "I apologise for Tukano." He started clapping his hands, and a few of the men joined in and they clapped until Mai Ranga said, "Ah, stop it all of you. Be useful men and buy more beer."

The men laughed. Then there was a moment of silence, which was broken by Mairosi saying to Mai Ranga, "You better do something

---

9   *muzukuru* — grandson or someone of that age to the speaker
10   *mbuya* — grandmother or someone of that age to the speaker

with that thing; his brother will be here soon; you know how he behaves when he has smoked his stuff."

"He's always like that," said VaChigero. "Something sure got in him in Joni."

"Leave Joni alone, people," said another man I had never seen before. "The spirits of dead soldiers have possessed him."

"Nonsense!" shouted Tukano. "I'm tired of people blaming the war for everything. War this, war that…I know—." Then he went quiet, as if he had forgotten what he wanted to say. Everyone was still looking at him, listening. He turned to Mai Ranga and said, "I think you should do something with that boy right away." Although my heart was beating hard, I felt better that he called me a boy, not a hare. He looked in the direction I had emerged from. His eyes were racing. I turned to see if they were seeing Mukoma, but I didn't see him. Still, I started to shudder as I thought of how he sometimes would always suddenly appear where I wasn't expecting him to be.

"Tukano is right," said VaChigero to Mai Ranga. "But what can you do with him though? What can anyone do?" He also peered in the direction of Chigorira Hill. "You know the brother will find the boy even if you hide him up your skirts."

A few men laughed.

"Nothing is funny!" shouted Mai Ranga, who tugged at my arm. "You, come!"

"Hide him well, and I don't mean just hiding. Think of something, hide him like a comrade," said VaChigero.

My head kept turning to Chigorira Hill. Then I saw Mukoma in the distance and heard Tukano say, "Better hurry up!" I struggled to free myself. I wanted to run to the stream and swim across the pond and vanish into the fields across. I struggled, turning, catching glimpses of Mukoma.

Several hands pulled me. My head kept turning; I didn't want it to, but it could not stop. Sometimes I saw, sometimes I didn't see Mukoma.

And the whole time my heart didn't stop kicking hard. A door opened and a man said, "Let me lift him, you hold the door."

"No, you hold the door," said Mai Ranga. "Hurry up!"

They lifted me. I kept turning to see if Mukoma had arrived. I felt Mukoma's presence not very far; I closed my eyes, but I still saw the image of Mukoma descending on me, the yellow of his shirt, the blue of his jeans; his boots hammering the ground; angry Mukoma raising his fists.

"Hey! Relax. We're trying to help you."

I struggled still. I was afraid they were going to keep holding me until Mukoma arrived. And then they would just hand me to him.

"Bring him in here," whispered Mai Ranga. "Madzvovera, hold that boy like a real man. Here!"

I was hauled into total darkness. But after a moment I noticed I was in a room. One of the men said, "There? Are you sure?"

"The brother would never guess, even if we let him search in here."

I turned my head to see where they were putting me. They dropped me into an empty grain barrel and I struggled, but it held me tightly in. Sitting in the drum felt like sinking. But I didn't want to struggle anymore. Now I understood they were trying to help me. I remained still, held my breath.

"Are we closing it?" said Mairosi.

"Let's close it," said another male voice.

"Hurry!" said Mai Ranga. "If he finds us outside, he'll not suspect a thing."

"But he may have already seen us coming in here."

"No, he was too far."

"But we saw him, which means he saw us."

"It's not that easy," said Mai Ranga. "Think like a man, Madzvovera."

I struggled again, I don't know why, hitting the sides of the drum with my elbows. I wanted to escape and continue running. They were trapping me; they were going to hand me to Mukoma in this drum.

"Hey!" said Mai Ranga. "Sit still in there if you want to live."

Deep in the container, darkness held its fists high.

"Close it tight. He's going to be fine," a man said.

"Leave the lid loose so he can breathe," Mai Ranga said; then there was a knock on the lid. "Point your nose to the top of the drum if you want to live. Do you hear?"

"Ye...e-s," I said, suppressing the urge to sneeze. I closed my eyes to avoid seeing the darkness. But the darkness I saw was even deeper, so I opened my eyes and focused on listening.

They asked each other whether Mukoma was nearby; then I heard them close the door noisily as they left the hut. I closed my eyes again. I didn't want fear to grip me.

A few moments later, the door banged open and I heard Mukoma saying, "You said you didn't see him at all?"

"Why would I have seen him?" Mai Ranga said in a low voice.

"I'm just asking." Pause. "And you're serious that he isn't in here somewhere?"

"Why would he be here?" asked Mai Ranga. "Is he my child?"

"Because if he is, there'll be trouble here."

"Says who?"

"So you want to play games with me now?" Mukoma boomed. "You do?"

"Don't you dare come near me, young man? Get away from near my hut too," said Mai Ranga. "Yes, I'm talking to you. I'm not one of your girlfriends. Move!"

"Listen, lady." Mukoma's voice was shaking again. "I have no time for nonsense."

"What?" said Mai Ranga. "Since when have I become your lady?" She went silent, then resumed. "We send you overseas and you come back calling us ladies! Is this what you call respect?"

"Mai Ranga, you will make me lose it!" shouted Mukoma. "South Africa is not overseas, and who gave you the idea that you sent me there?"

I heard the stamping of feet on the ground; then laughter from the fire. Silence. Then one man said, "Jeri, I know you have a right to beat the boy anytime, but you're crossing the line here. You can't talk like that to Mai Ranga, who is like your aunt."

"Bugger off, man!" shouted Mukoma. I could picture his hands forming into big fists.

"Who're you calling *man*?" asked the man at the fire. "I who is like a brother to your mother? I who saw you growing up? I who helps your mother with her fieldwork? And all you call me is *man*?" That was VaNgeya, the old man who always visited Mother.

Another shuffle signalled the arrival of someone. Mai Ranga coughed. Then I heard a third male voice saying, "We know you're a grown-up, the more reason you shouldn't waste your time chasing a boy around."

Mukoma said, "Listen, Tukano, you've no right to meddle in my business."

"So you have a business and I'm the middleman?" Pause. "Then I just got hired on the spot, people."

There was laughter from — I think — the fire. Even Mai Ranga coughed out a brief laugh. Then she said, "You men, there's beer to be drunk, and money to exchange hands. Let's get moving." I heard footsteps shuffling away.

"You too Jeri, give us that Joni money!" There was silence. "Ah! Where do you think you're going?" She didn't receive an answer. "Who are you to try to sneak into an old woman's private hut and think you can get away with it?"

"If you're lying to me there'll be trouble here. I want to search on my own," Mukoma said.

"I don't see that happening!" said Mai Ranga. "*Shuwa*-o,[11] you would've to beat me first."

"Just watch." Then the door swung open again, but someone tried to close it, then it banged against the wall. The light from outside lit the inside of the drum, but, holding my breath, I didn't move.

"Don't get in there, or I'll take off my clothes, *shuwa*-o," Mai Ranga said.

"No, you'll not do that… Ah, hey, what do you think you're doing?" Mukoma's voice had taken a worried tone.

"I told you, didn't I? How would you feel if I came and tried to force my way into your bedroom hut?"

Several voices grumbled and the loudest said, "Jeri, you're playing with fire now!"

Mukoma remained silent. I waited for Mai Ranga's voice. It didn't come, but the man at the fire said, "Some things just let go! The comrades get time to play, even when they know the soldiers are nearby."

"Your point?" said Mukoma.

"You can't live like this, young man," said VaChigero. "And why are you so angry? What did they do to you in South Africa?"

Mukoma didn't answer. The door was closed and I heard Mukoma's boots walking away. There was silence, then a big sigh from Mai Ranga.

"Mairosi, your friend didn't answer VaChigero's question," she said.

"You saw the dark cloud on his face?"

"He should've joined the comrades," said VaChigero. "He needs a real war, with a gun."

"But that doesn't make sense. He carves stools; helps his mother," said Mairosi.

"It's the war, that's what I say. Look at the evil filling up the bellies of our daughters," VaChigero said. Indeed, he had a whole kraal of daughters.

---

11   *Shuwa-o* — a Shona phonological corruption of the word sure. Then with addition of -o, it means surely/truly

"But is that what's making him beat the boy every day?"

"Maybe," said Mairosi, "but don't they say Shami ran away with a comrade?"

"Shami did what?"

"Tukano, don't act like you don't live in Mhototi," said Mairosi.

"So what does that mean?" asked Mai Ranga.

"Ah, where have you been, Mai Ranga? Aren't you this village's radio?"

"But I don't know what Shami has to do with him beating this orphan."

"Well, she was already pregnant when she slept with that comrade."

"What?" said Mai Ranga. "Jeri used to play with Shami?"

"Play? Ha. Ha. Ha. You must mean *play*."

"*Hezvo, nhai vedu!*"[12] said Mai Ranga. "This war is evil."

They went silent as if they were looking at the evil drifting across the sky. I shifted in the drum and listened closely. I could see my toes now.

"He refused to marry her, so she found a comrade." That was VaChigero again. "The comrade sent her to his village. Even comrades can be stupid too."

"That's a story," said Mai Ranga. "But I don't want him to continue beating this boy though."

"Like he said, let him do his job of raising the boy," said Tukano. "We were all raised like that."

"Since when does *mbanje*[13] raise a person?"

"*Mbanje*? What are you talking about now?"

"Come on, you saw his eyes."

"But still..."

"Yeah, he just needs to grow up; to get married or something."

"Tukano, didn't you just hear what we said about Shami?"

---

12   *Hezvo, nhai vedu!* - a cry of helplessness, enlisting sympathy or help.
13   *mbanje* - marijuana or dagga

"Who cares about Shami? The village is suffocating with young women."

On and on, they talked, their voices growing fainter and fainter. I sat in the drum, tears burning my eyes. I wasn't thinking about Mukoma anymore, I wasn't afraid even. One day I would grow up to join the war and kill that comrade. Shami had always taken me to the stores, buying me sweets, cooking for me when she came to visit Mukoma, back when he laughed a lot. She had just suddenly vanished, and Mukoma had not told me what happened.

I wasn't thinking anymore. I just sat in the drum, listening to fragments of their conversation. Every now and then I heard other sounds, the chirping of birds, the braying of a donkey, and the bleating of a goat. At one point, I heard a sound in the room too, a crawling, perhaps of a rat, but I ignored it; in fact, I didn't want to think of the possibility of the presence of something dangerous, a snake, a scorpion. But Mai Ranga had many cats, so rats and snakes were not likely to be her problem.

I strained to catch more fragments of what they were saying. Then I heard Mai Ranga say, "Let's finish up. I have to go to the field tomorrow."

"We thank you our keeper," said Tukano's voice.

Other voices expressed gratitude in like manner, and then they faded away in the distance. But one more male voice, VaChigero's said, "You don't need company tonight?"

"There's a boy here. Don't you have any sense?"

"Will you let the boy go?"

"Sure. He'll go."

"So what's the problem?"

"He'll sleep here. I want to punish the brother, crazy man. People who don't grow up."

"Some of us are grown," said VaChigero, clearing his throat.

"Find your way home." There was a pause. "Wives are waiting."

"Did you have to go there?"

"I just did."

Then, coughing, VaChigero left. I could hear the sounds of Mai Ranga putting away things. I sat waiting for her to tell me what to do next, but when her sounds faded too, I curled in the barrel to settle into comfort. That was when the wound on my foot started to sting, and my anger at Mukoma rose again.

The Vessel

Although I was too young to be possessed, Mai sent letters to Mukoma the year I started belching. The first letter read: *'Anodzvova[14] every day for hours, and when he stops, he is too tired to do any work, so I let him sleep, even in daytime, to allow the spirits to make up their minds. Please come home with speed. Come, my son, so we can run around to find out what we need to do to appease the ancestors.'* Mai was saying the words while I wrote, but, belching the whole time, I took long to finish writing the letter.

I was not eager to get possessed yet, but should it happen, I knew I would enjoy seeing grown-ups gathering to clap their hands and listen to the spirit speaking through me. As a medium, or what the villagers called *homwe* — vessel — I would tell them what to do. I would be the first among my friends to get possessed, thus gaining fame in all of Mhototi and other villages of Mazvihwa. I would be famous in the whole world, no doubt.

Mai wanted the letter to be clear, to make Mukoma travel home soon after reading it. He alone had the authority to direct my possession rituals. We shared the same father, and our totem was different from that of the rest of the extended family.

The thought of a spirit seizing me made my heart pound, and my belching intensified, causing Mai to speak with an urgency of one terrified, but hers was a kind of happy terror. If I ended up getting possessed by my father's spirit, my father who had died eleven years earlier, Mai would have a chance to hear her husband's voice again.

After checking the letter for errors, I stood up to fetch an envelope, but Mai told me to sit down and write some more: *'He also says his sides hurt, so I am sure your father's spirit is finally thinking of returning.*

---

14   *Anodzvova* - he belches (as a sign marking the beginnings of spirit possession as noted in Shona culture)

There is no time to waste. The signs are clear, and questions that we have asked for many years are finally getting answered. Come home, my son; come so we can run around and see what we can find.'

When she paused, I touched my left side to feel the pain. It hurt, so I knew the other side would start hurting soon. These things happened all the time. When Tukano lost his job and came to the village belching and complaining about the pain in his ribs, it only took a week for him to get possessed. In another case, Mateni, who ignored the signs when his wife and child fell sick, learned the hard way not to ignore the ancestors. When he became ill too, he told people he would just jog and regain his fitness, but within a day he couldn't walk, and when he stopped talking altogether, his relatives invited a *n'anga*[15] from Takavarasha. Mateni was possessed within a week and the illness left his family.

I thought we were done writing the letter and was getting excited about sealing it in the envelope when Mai told me to take a walk or just play outside while she thought of more things to say. A matter like this, she said, needed people, referring to herself, to think hard, and to choose their words carefully so that other people, talking about Mukoma, would see its importance and act promptly. I had my own thinking to do too. Perhaps the spirits would make me a healer, which would mean that, at age eleven, I would be the youngest person in Mhototi to start earning a living as a *n'anga*.

Outside, the sun looked possessed; red, it sat on the Vhugwi Mountains like an ignorant bull. He seemed to think the world was just about him and not about everyone else, not about me, not about Mai or about Mukoma. I ignored the sinking sun and, belching uncontrollably, walked to Chomumbuyu Hill on the eastern side of our home. I sat on a large rock and imagined my future of spiritual success. Even when I tried to fight the urge, the belching attacked like a storm. This was a

---

15   *n'anga* - Shona term for traditional healer/diviner

good sign. We really needed to finish writing the letter and send it to Harare as soon as possible.

I pictured Mukoma opening the letter with eager hands, and then smiling as he started reading, happy that his little brother was going to be possessed and become a vessel. Vessels were different from ordinary people; we were powerful, gifted and respected. Most families in Mhototi had an adult vessel. Child vessels were rare, so I was going to make our family famous. Why even the whole family? I was going to be the famous one, and all the other boys my age would die of jealousy. As for the girls, they would start flocking to me. I would probably be married by the time I turned sixteen.

I say family, but the word makes me shudder whenever I use it. What I call our family consisted only of Mukoma and me. Even though we were part of the big extended family, to which we were connected through Mai, in matters of ancestral worship we were a two-member family. Mai, as a woman, couldn't play an important role in these matters. Mukoma and I shared the same father, but he also belonged to the extended family because he shared his mother, Mai, with four half-brothers. My own mother had died a month after giving birth to me, so I called Mai my mother. I doubted that she thought I knew that she was not my real mother since whenever she whipped me for misbehaving, she would remind me that no child who had come from her womb should misbehave, and the more she mentioned her womb the harder she would lash at me. I liked to hear her telling me I had come from her womb, and it made the beatings less painful. And now, I could see Mai was going to make sure Mukoma would do what he needed to do for me to get possessed.

Mukoma had already tried to get possessed many times, as everyone expected, especially the year he returned from South Africa after losing his job. People had gathered at our home and danced, but no spirit possessed him. The drums had wailed and there had been dancing until the earthen floor started to crack, but still, no spirit came. As Mukoma hammered the floor with his bare feet, the crowd clapped harder to bring him closer to possession. He sweated and ran out of breath, and, instead of the spirit possessing him, he got the hiccups and fell down. Some people thought he was possessed and they crowded around him, but he struggled to his knees and said, "Fuck!" Some asked what he was saying, and others replied that he was angry about something. The crowd stopped clapping altogether, and two men helped him to his feet and told him to continue trying. Mukoma raised an open hand and said, "How about we stop trying?" He left the dancing circle and limped outside, leaving the elders open-mouthed. Later, he told me that if he was not the chosen one, then one of us was — and there were only the two of us.

****

Back home, I found Mai ready to finish the letter. We added these details: *"After you read this letter, think about what we have always said about your father. It has been many years since he passed away and I am sure he is unhappy that no one is doing his work. So, please, do something, finish reading this letter and come home right away. Greet others there, and when you come home bring them with you."* This was her way of reminding Mukoma to bring his girlfriend, Juliet, whom most people in the village already referred to as his wife. They lived together in Harare. Mai said it was not good for them to continue living together without getting married first.

On the next day, a Tuesday, we sent the first letter with Magi, our neighbour's daughter who worked as a maid in Harare. She promised to deliver it on the same day, so Mai and I expected Mukoma to plan his trip home on the weekend or even sooner, to take me to a *n'anga* who would work on my case and train me. We could visit several of them in Mazvihwa and Mberengwa. There was Madzvovera of Chishamba, just across the river from our village, who was good with possession and witchcraft matters. I could also be taken to Chikwati of Murowa, the best in herbs and madness. He had treated Patson Dzenga, the man who had woken up one day and smeared himself with his waste and ran down the village telling people that he was the new angel of ghosts. His family consulted four *n'angas*, three prophets, and visited the clinic at Mapaire, but Dzenga worsened, and when he began eating his *tsvina*,[16] they took him to Chikwati, and within a week he became normal again.

If Mukoma would not agree to visit the local diviners, we could go to Mberengwa to see a famous old woman who knew your names even before you arrived in her compound. She mixed traditional healing and Zion spirituality, switching from Zion prophecy to Karanga divination, depending on what her patients wanted. She lived on the summit of Bhuchwa Mountain, close to a sacred pond known throughout Zimbabwe and the whole world. Because of the sacred nature of Bhuchwa, those who planned to visit the woman had to consult with other *n'angas* first to be instructed on how to behave in front of her.

The first weekend came and went without a sign of Mukoma. And the belching continued. Whenever it stopped, Mai and I were worried, but then it would start again and continue for hours, and Mai would say, "So now where is he? Isn't he the one who named you after your father?" The name, as Mai had explained many times, came with responsibilities; I could easily continue father's spiritual work, if his spirit would choose me for the role. And now we had the signs.

When the belching stopped for a whole day, Mai had a talk with me.

"What's wrong with you?" she asked.

I shook my head and said, "Nothing is wrong."

"Obviously something is, otherwise you wouldn't just stop," she said. "Remember, we already sent a letter to your brother."

I sat with my head cast down, afraid that Mai felt I was letting her down. I was letting myself down too. I was letting down everyone, the

---

16   *tsvina* - human waste

whole of Mhototi, the whole of Zimbabwe, the whole world, by not remaining ready for the ancestors to choose me.

Within hours, I started belching again. In fact, for the rest of the week, the belching did not stop for long periods of time.

But Mukoma did not come.

We wrote the second letter on Saturday evening, which went like this: *"Hurry, please hurry. Why do you remain quiet like you didn't read what I wrote in my last letter? These things are not things to play with. Come, please come, and we will take him to Madzvovera, and if you want, to the Razor Woman in Bhuchwa."* I wrote and belched, and Mai said, "Write that too; tell him that you are belching as you write." I hesitated; then I did it: *"As he writes this letter, he is belching. You must remember that being his elder brother, you are the head of the family, and this is something to help your family and its future."* We sent the letter with Mudamburi's son, who worked in a bakery in Chitungwiza, near Harare.

Another weekend came and went and still there was no sign of Mukoma. Already, I had missed three days of school, and I was having dreams in which I flew over rivers, always landing on father's talking grave, where if I lingered longer, a wild pig always emerged and chased me away. That's when I would wake up drenched in sweat, my heart pounding. When I told Mai about my dreams, we wrote another letter: *"How is work over there? Are the whites treating you well? Did you get that stand for a house that you said you were going to buy? Is your female friend thinking of visiting us soon? We waited all of last week, and the one before, for your arrival. His signs are not stopping, and he is growing thinner."*

Mai asked me if I wanted to add a question too, and I told her I just wanted to tell Mukoma that this year the baobab trees were being generous, that I had stored heaps of baobabs to last me a whole year, but Mai said Mukoma would not find that interesting; I should just tell him that his cow, Harare, had given birth. I had already named the calf

Bulawayo because we had learned in Geography that it was the second largest city of Zimbabwe. Mai had named the cow Harare because Mukoma had bought it with money he had earned in Harare, which she said would multiply once the cow started bearing calves. I wrote the detail about the birth, and even added that if he didn't like the name Bulawayo, it was not too late to give it another one, maybe Mashava, the town he had his first job. *"The calf is brown but it has a white spot shaped like a map on its face,"* I wrote. When I read it aloud to Mai, she disapproved.

"I didn't say get into all that! Just telling him there's a calf was enough," she said.

"I can cross it out," I said, poising the pen.

"No, don't. The words came from your heart, right?"

"Deep down."

"Then leave them there. We want to keep this letter clean." She folded her arms on her lap and averted her eyes to the roof. *"I don't mean to bother you. I know you are very busy, but the matter at hand needs you here."*

I looked at her and she understood that I was about to ask a question, so she gave the answer, "I don't want to anger him before he even makes up his mind. He's a good son who sends me groceries and money, and takes care of you like a father."

"Maybe he's on a bus right now," I said.

"He better be," she said, "I can't do anything about this without him."

As if to confirm that something needed to be done soon, another belch gathered within me and I let it out.

We travelled to Takavarasha Township to post the third letter. It was my first time to see a real mailbox, which made me think that when I dropped the letter in, it was as if I was throwing it away, but Mai nodded at me and said, "It will get there." She said maybe the previous letters had not been delivered, but posting the letter this way would ensure no one would lose it.

She showed me Mugwebi Store and Butchery, where father had once worked at as a tailor. "That was many years ago, long before we knew you would be born," she said. We were standing on the veranda, not very far from the corner used by the current tailor. I wanted to go inside the store, but Mai said, "No one will remember him now. Don't waste your time asking." I just wanted to stand in the store and think about him, try to imagine what he had looked like. I stared at the empty tailor's chair and the sewing machine instead, which was covered in canvas. I wondered how soon the current tailor would return from his break or lunch, or wherever he had gone.

"Do you think he may remember Father?" I asked, but Mai started walking away. I gave the red chair one more look, and followed her.

On the way home I could not stop thinking about Father — what type of man he had been, what he had looked like, what plans he had had for me, what his last words had been. The thing I always thought about was how his life had been in Mozambique when he was a boy. I wanted to know when he had found out that he was a spirit medium, whether that had happened when he was still in Mozambique, or after he came to Zimbabwe. No one knew these details; neither Mukoma nor Mai talked about these things, just as they did not talk about the specific circumstances of my own birth, how Father had met my mother, when he had left his wife, and what had happened that caused my mother to die a month after giving birth to me. Once, when I asked to see photos of Father, Mai had said there weren't any, there hadn't been any, but I would find out years later that she had burned all of them when Father died.

We waited for another week, but, although the belching didn't stop, Mukoma didn't come. By now, other people in Mhototi were aware of my condition. VaNgeya,[17] the old man who came to talk to Mai every morning, said we should not jump to conclusions. He said maybe I was

---

17   VaNgeya - Mr Ngeya

making myself belch to be allowed to miss school. "You know with these young ones, once they see a fault in your judgement, they stretch your patience like rubber," he said. But Mai shook her head and said nothing. She knew something that VaNgeya couldn't—wouldn't— understand, no matter how hard he tried. He couldn't get it, we didn't care much if he did; we knew what we knew, Mai and I. We were more like a team.

At school, I always muffled the belching so as not to invite laughter from other pupils. I also didn't want to get in trouble for making noise in class. Once, when a bout caught me unawares, the class burst out laughing, but the teacher silenced everyone and joked, "Maybe he has a *sekuru*[18] trying to possess him." He walked over to me, and said, "Do you?" But I remembered Mai had said I couldn't tell anyone at school yet, nor was I supposed to tell my friends, so I just shook my head no, while chewing my lips, and the teacher left me alone. I am glad he left me alone; sometimes if you disrespected a spirit medium, bad things could happen to you, even if you were a teacher. I knew that he would find out soon that I was a special person, a chosen of the spirit world. Everyone in my class would. I just knew it.

In the fourth letter, we asked Mukoma if he had seen the other three. If he had not seen them, here was the message again: *'Fati now bleeds through the nose and he has a headache almost every day. We already wrote about how he was belching day and night, and we thought maybe the spirits were ready for him. I thought after three letters you would say, "Maybe, Mai has something important to say and I must go home today." Even Fati thought you would be here by now. A thing like this cannot be delayed.'*

Mai told me to add that asking Mukoma to come home was not meant to disturb him from his important work in Harare, we all benefited from the groceries and the money he sent every month, but it was a

_____

18   *sekuru* - male ancestor/grandfather

way of following the wishes of the ancestors, carried in the signs — the headache, the nosebleed, the belching, and the rib pains. We concluded the letter in this way: *'Hurry so we can go to Madzvovera. That's the only way we can know what the spirits want. He misses school often these days. And I am afraid that if they visit him while he is at school, there will be no one to talk to them and they may become too angry. An angry ancestor is not easy to appease.'*

That moved me, and I could feel tears burning in my eyes. I hoped Mukoma would feel the same way after reading it, but when he didn't come home the following weekend, Mai said we were done writing letters. "Do you still feel tired?" she asked.

"On and off all the time," I said.

I felt weak in the mornings and late at night, like someone was sitting on my shoulders. My headaches attacked the forehead area, and the nosebleeds sometimes attacked me at night. I sweated a lot too, and sometimes had difficulty breathing. Mai became restless. All day, she sighed and sneezed, and I could tell by her humming that she was planning something serious, something that would not involve Mukoma.

That evening we visited Madzvovera. No dogs barked when we arrived at the *n'anga*'s homestead. A little girl in an oversized brown dress that looked like a sack guided us to a small, dim hut that smelt of snuff tobacco, where the *n'anga* sat waiting for us. As soon as we entered the hut, the girl bolted out. Two women sat on either side of the mysterious Madzvovera, and a boy my age sat beating a small drum in tune to the women's singing. The *n'anga* was adorned in an animal skin overcoat, and a sparsely feathered headdress, but I also saw that he had trousers on, for I had expected that his whole body would be covered in animal fur. When we were seated, the singing increased and the little drum wailed. I saw stacks of boxes against the back wall, the hut's two triangular windows without panels, the flower patterns painted in white on the brown wall, and in front of the *n'anga* was a little circle drawn on the floor in two lines of black and white chalk. I could sense the presence of spirits in the hut, and as the singing and the drumming continued, the sounds felt like they were coming from within me. By my side, Mai sat silently, hands clasped together. Following her example, I clasped my hands too, but she saw and unclasped hers. I returned my attention to the *n'anga*.

Madzovera's eyes darted in our direction and he started to quiver, exactly what I had expected him to do. I sat up straight to observe him closely, but I couldn't tell if he was looking at us, or at the door behind us, which was half-open to let in some light. Then he closed his eyes, jerked his body, and soon he was belching and coughing. Suddenly, he went still, flashed his eyes open, and I knew the spirit had arrived, had taken over.

My skin crawled. Mai started to clap. The singing and the drumming ceased, and the spirit, speaking through Madzvovera said, "I saw you coming!" Madzvovera's eyes widened to emphasize the seeing. "Something is wrong!"

Mai leaned forward and, while clapping, said, "Yes, Ancient One. He who has walked has what has troubled his heart."

My hair bristled and my head shook as my eyes met those of the medium. The spirit made Madzvovera blink furiously. He roared, contorted his face, and tilted his head like he was in pain. He leaned sideways and roared again. I almost jumped up, but I resettled to avoid attracting his attention. I didn't want him to talk to me directly, yet I didn't want him to think I wasn't interested in possession. I leaned forward like Mai, my elbows on my thighs.

Madzvovera let out another deep belch, fixed his gaze on Mai and said, "What brings you here, *chizukuru!*"[19]

Mai explained to the spirit that she had brought me to open the way for the ancestors to start their work, that she thought I was showing the signs and she had no doubt I was being called to something important, but what did she know, being a person of flesh and a woman only, she

---

19   *chizukuru* - grandchild who is small in stature/age

48

might be wrong, which is why she had dragged me here, emphasis on that word, dragged.

Then there was singing as the *n'anga* roared and shook his head. For a moment I was scared, but I had to show courage and readiness. I sat still and started clapping my hands in tune with the singing and the coughs of the little drum. On cue, the singing stopped, and the *n'anga* said, "So you think he is the one?" His eyes stabbed Mai. "You must know he is the one?"

"We don't know, Ancient One, but we are here for your guidance," Mai said. "It is only a fool who seeks to guide himself when the world is full of wisdom of the ancestors."

There was a moment of silence, which was followed by the sudden boom of the small drum. The boy was beating the drum as if he was possessed too, and one of the women produced a sudden trill of ululation. Excitement rose in my heart, and I could feel my stomach tighten. This was the life I was going to lead. I was staring at the red eyes of my future. Madzvovera was going to train me, make me the best *n'anga* in Mazvihwa as he was already the best in Chivi.

"We know he's the one," said Madzvovera. "We just want to tell you what needs to be done." He finished a belch that had not quite begun. I restrained my own, which had started to build up. I couldn't help but admire how Madzvovera was referring to himself as "we". Indeed, a sign of power. Even Mai stopped clapping and watched Madzvovera shaking. The women resumed singing. But they stopped immediately when the spirit groaned.

"Do you want him to run like lightning or to croak like a frog?" the spirit asked.

"Only you the Great One can give us speed," Mai said in a soft voice. "We want the wonders of our world to begin lighting to make skies smile."

"You came to the right place." I couldn't tell if it was the spirit who had said this, or if it was Madzvovera himself. I didn't know if possession took over the whole person, or if a part of you was always there, talking when the spirit was silent.

"Yes, we did," Mai said, then she dug me with her elbow and I started clapping as well. The *n'anga* pulled a small, black sack from behind him, untied its neck and emptied the contents on the floor. Three cockroaches crawled out and started advancing towards me. But they stopped in the little circle drawing in front of the *n'anga;* then crawled towards each other until their heads touched. With widening eyes, I looked at them as they flicked their tiny antennae. I thought I was dreaming, but I didn't take my eyes from the creatures, which had stopped moving altogether. They seemed to know what I was thinking. I looked up and my eyes met Madzvovera's.

The *n'anga* groaned. "Where is he, this vessel?" he asked, his stare directed towards the door again, the eyes with the same distant look which I had seen before Madzvovera was possessed: squinted dark, distant pits pondering. "Where is the one you think is the one?" the *n'anga* asked again, urgency in his voice.

I wanted to raise my hand like I was in class, but I looked at Mai. She opened her mouth and then closed it, as if this was the first time she was talking to a *n'anga*. "You are looking at him, Great One," she said finally, pointing at me.

"No, we don't see him here," the spirit said. "The one we ought to be looking at is somewhere afar."

"But this one belches!" Mai said. She had suddenly raised her voice.

"He belches?" Madzovera asked, looking surprised. "Who belches?"

"This one here; all the time," said Mai leaning forward. "On and off all the time."

Madzvovera groaned and looked at Mai, at me, then at Mai again.

"Yes, *sekuru*,[20] what is it?" asked Mai.

"You have a vessel in the family; a big vessel," he said. "You have a vessel, and his thorn bushes need to be felled for the millet to be planted

---

20   *sekuru* - grandfather or traditional healer or mother's father or mother's brother
      (depending on the context.) Here, it is a traditional healer/diviner.

50

by season's time." He twisted his face as if unlocking a truth deep within, then, when his face had calmed, he guided the roaches back into the bag, and my heart sank. There had to be something wrong in how the roaches had failed to detect my presence, or whatever message they had given the *n'anga*, I just knew they could not be right. I could feel a little anger gripping my cheeks.

"You have a big vessel somewhere," Madzvovera said, after one of the women took the roach sack from him.

"Yes, that's why we came here," said Mai. "We came to receive your wisdom."

"But what kind of hunter hunts without a dog?" Madzvovera asked.

"I brought the little dog with me, *sekuru*."

He sniffed the thick air and looked at me with dead eyes. Then he jumped up and landed in a crouch. The *n'anga* looked at Mai and said, "Go back and when you return bring the real vessel." He belched and started a low laugh that ended as a growl. "Once you bring him, your soil will listen."

The drum boy handed him a snuff container, and before opening it, Madzvovera quivered, belched and groaned. He quivered a little longer as Mai clapped harder. After a brief moment of quivering, he looked at us with a softer expression. It became clear that the spirit had left. Madzvovera turned to the older of the women and said, "Did they get what they travelled for?"

"They were told to come back again, with the older brother."

Madzvovera looked at Mai and said, "So yes, just do as they said: that's what we of the flesh do when the spirit world speaks..."

Mai nodded, looking at the floor. "The spirits, so it shall be as they said, but I can't find the courage to fight the confusion that sits in my chest." Mai sat up and sighed. "It's just that this one is showing the signs."

"The works of the ancestors sometimes come in riddles," said Madzvovera, who then chuckled, rubbing his palms together.

Mai didn't say anything. I avoided Madzvovera's eyes.

"Feed the tin and walk away with feet that will remember the path that leads back here," said Madzvovera, pinching his snuff with three fingers, and as he brought the fingers to his nose, he watched Mai put some money in a black tin that one of the women held towards us. When the bills were in the tin, Madzvovera sniffed loudly and sneezed.

Shortly after, we walked out of the hut and Mai talked with Madzovera some more, asking about ordinary matters like the rains and how his crops were doing. We didn't stay for the food we were offered as Mai said we needed to get home before it was too dark. I knew she was afraid of the ghosts for which the path from this place to our home was known.

We didn't talk to each other until we arrived at home, but I could hear Mai's heavy breathing, which competed with mine. I thought at any moment I would see a short, white figure emerging out of the bushes. Mai kept looking, casting glances at the bushes too, but she didn't say anything, didn't even hum, which she often did when she was afraid.

As we entered our homestead, she said, "He failed to see."

I agreed, but I didn't know how to say so.

"Who can fail to see the signs? Even a blind person will see that you have something on your shoulders."

I touched my shoulders. I too had no idea why Madzvovera's spirit had not seen the spirit sitting on my shoulders. Or, was I too young to have anything seen on me? This spirit world was becoming confusing to me.

In the kitchen hut Mai said, "We will give your brother another week, and if he doesn't come, we go there to Harare."

My heart beat faster. That would be my first trip to Harare. And no other boy or girl in Mhototi had ever travelled there either. At eleven years old, I would be the youngest Mhototi boy to go to Harare.

"Harare?" I gasped, only it came out as a belch.

Mai nodded and said, "We might have to do that. There are *n'angas* there too. And you deserve the help of someone who knows what he is doing."

True, Madzvovera had wasted our time.

I was ready for new things, looking forward to travelling to Harare. Maybe Mukoma would decide to keep me there, enrol me in a new school and allow me to live with him in the city. I would be the first boy from Mhototi to attend school in Harare and that would make me so popular that I would get a girlfriend, like Obert who attended school in Bulawayo and only came to the village on holidays. Tsitsi, his girlfriend, lived in the village and talked incessantly about all sorts of things Obert brought her. She never stopped talking about Bulawayo. I too would have a girlfriend who would always talk about Harare.

****

In three days, we received a letter from Mukoma. He knew that I had missed school, and he was not happy about it. He was planning to come home next weekend, to "fix" me, which I understood to mean a thorough beating. Didn't I remember what he had told me about the importance of education? How he had said nothing else but school would raise our family from poverty? I could feel the anger of his words as I read them. My heart beat faster and fear gripped me, especially when I read these words: *You will see me when I arrive.*

Mai listened, her mouth opening wider, as if she had seen a ghost. She raised her hand for me to stop reading. "That's why I think Madzvovera let us down," she said. "Your brother is not serious, and something evil has seized and blinded him." She twisted her lips and looked away, her eyes directed to Chomumbuyu Hill. I looked in that direction, my stare resting on the white rock outcrops that had once scared me when I was small, when I had thought they were poised to grab me.

Mai sat like that for a while. When her steady gaze was on me again, she said, "Let him try to touch you again when he gets here and he will see how I don't care that he is a grown man."

I belched. It had come stealthily and caught me by surprise. Mai nodded and said, "Read."

"Tell Mai that either you or I will be possessed when the right time comes, and the right time for you is when you have learned, until there is nothing left in books to learn."

When I looked up, I found Mai already shaking with anger.

"Do you want me to read it again?" I asked.

She shook her head and waved me away. As I stood up and entered the kitchen hut, I was thinking of getting some drinking water, but I picked a book instead and left for Chomumbuyu, where I would perch on the white rocks to read and belch in private.

The Bull of Mhototi

Axes dangling from our shoulders, we walked briskly towards Chimhiti forest to cut down trees to obtain poles for a granary Mukoma wanted to build before he returned to Harare. I followed closely behind him, trying to keep up with his pace, until I was panting by his side. He slowed down, and while looking at Maregere, a tree-netted hill on the right side of the path, said, "So Fati, do you think you are a good fighter like me?"

"Yes, no doubt," I said, and he laughed. I looked at the hill too, where startled doves exploded from the *jarakamba*[1] trees at the foot of the hill. I wished I had brought my catapult.

"So can you beat Simba in a fist-fight?" Mukoma asked.

"Any day, any minute," I said, but I knew I was no match for Simba. He would just knock me out, roast me, and throw me to the dogs. "That one is a coward, and he fears even my shadow."

"Good!" said Mukoma, nodding. "Now that's my man." He patted me on the shoulders.

If I admitted that Simba could beat me, Mukoma would easily call me a coward and maybe start beating me himself. He smoked *mbanje,* and whenever I upset him, no one could stop him from squashing me like a cockroach. But I wanted to grow up and be like him.

"What is our totem again?" he always asked me.

"Lion," I would say.

"And what are we full of?"

"Might and courage," I would say, beaming.

He would nod and smile proudly. I had never seen him lose in a fight. When he was in the village, he fought a lot, and people called him the bull of Mhototi. His presence made other men behave.

---

1   *jarakamba* - an indigenous tree in Zimbabwe

Two days earlier, he had knocked down Tukano, the village brute, at Vhazhure Beer Hall. Tukano always attacked people when he was drunk. He had fought in the war of liberation in the 1970s, but people told him they didn't care about that war anymore, so he beat them up, calling himself Hamayeropa (friend of blood), his war name. Mukoma had given him a good beating though, and as his war name implied, Hamayeropa had befriended blood. This was the most talked about fight in Mhototi.

As I thought about the fight, I smiled and said, "Simba can never say *pwe-e*[2] to me."

"How come?" Mukoma asked.

"I would blast him." I shook a fist in the air.

Mukoma laughed briefly; I just had used his favourite word. "Of course, you can blast him; you have my courage."

My skin crawled, and I felt like I belonged to a special club of fighters, consisting of only Mukoma and me. I laughed at the possibility of actually beating Simba until he soiled himself; then my heart started beating faster, when my mind wandered to Simba's fight with Ndudzo, the week before, in Teacher Mangena's garden.

We were cultivating and watering the vegetable beds, plucking out rotting or wilting leaves. The work was going on smoothly with everyone focused on their tasks. Then Ndudzo looked at Simba's hoe and burst out laughing. Everyone stopped working.

"What?" asked Simba, with his impatient, warrior's voice.

"People whose fathers don't work in towns have sickly hoes," said Ndudzo, "hoes that cannot cut the weakest weed on earth." He then continued laughing, his face tilted to the sky.

Simba's neck swelled like a puff adder's. He jumped from his stoop, landed close to Ndudzo's feet, and said, "Children of witches have rotten mouths. They spit stinky words." He bent down again and

---

2   *pwe-e* - a Shona ideophone uttered by someone who is provoking his/her opponent into a fight

resumed his work while the class laughed. It thrilled us to hear that Ndudzo's mother was a witch who rode on a hyena and went hunting for human flesh at night. Some started showering insults on Ndudzo, who began wilting with shame.

Simba glared at Ndudzo again and shouted, "Son of a *muroyi!*"[3]

"Whose mother is a *muroyi*, you fool?" Ndudzo said, lips trembling. He dashed closer to Simba.

Silence descended on us. We gasped when Ndudzo raised a fist and shook it in Simba's face. There surely was something wrong with Ndudzo; no one challenged Simba that way.

We formed a ring around them.

"Your mother is a witch and she takes you along on her night trips," Simba said, then addressing the crowd, he shouted, "We have a goblin among us!"

We cheered and stamped the ground with our feet.

When silence returned, Ndudzo broke into a laugh that made his body quiver and double over; then he threw his hoe onto the ground, and said, "It's not your fault that you're poor. That little hoe is because your father fears work. That's exactly why he was fired. Now he goes around telling people his company closed. Lies!" He resumed his loud laugh, which made some of us laugh too. "Very soon, you'll be kicked out of school, you little," he hesitated, "chicken!"

"Ah!" we said. We couldn't believe what Ndudzo had just said. He burst out laughing again, head tilted helplessly to the side.

Simba leapt forward, landing dangerously close to Ndudzo.

We drew closer to see the blow that would knock Ndudzo out, but Simba did not strike. Instead, he gave a nasty little smile, swaggered, and said, "It's not your fault that your mother is a witch. It's not hers either. She just finds human flesh delicious. And you, you just eat what's

---

3   *muroyi* - witch/wizard

put in front of you, what choice have you got?" Simba then turned to us, tossed a fist in the air and shouted, "Ndudzo eats people!"

"Ndudzo eats people!" we shouted back.

Ndudzo gazed at the ground, his hand holding his chin. We looked there too, wondering what he was seeing. Even Simba seemed not to know what to do next, but because he was Simba, he repeated his chant and the crowd responded, louder. Our excitement rose like a gust of wind looking for a fire to enrage. And Simba started to dance the *kongonya*[4] dance around Ndudzo to show his quick dismissal of him as an opponent. Some in the crowd joined in the dancing, skipping, jumping, round and round.

Then Ndudzo struck — a backhander that tore Simba's lip. All motion ceased and we stood shocked. The metallic smell of blood filled the air. Even Ndudzo looked surprised by the impact of his own slap, but the crowd wanted him to do more. Girls ululated while boys whistled and punched the air with their fists. We sang Ndudzo's name.

Simba's hands formed into huge chunks of fists that could scare even an adult. He raised one fist and advanced towards Ndudzo, but Aaron, the class monitor, blocked the blow before it hit Ndudzo's forehead. He planted himself between the two, and we murmured in disapproval. Our shouts rose like thunder when Aaron made a 'no-fighting' sign with his open palm, but he waited for the noise to die down.

"I'm not trying to stop the fight," Aaron said. "We're here, the teachers are there." He pointed to the staff room "Those who want to fight can fight!"

We clapped our hands, whistled or ululated. We wanted to see bleeding noses and swelling faces, torn lips and bruised knees. Squashed running noses too!

---

4   *kongonya* - a type of dance characterised by front and back movement of the waist and rhythmic jumping which was created in Zimbabwe during the liberation struggle. In this instance, the dance is used as a provoking tool.

"As with every fight," resumed Aaron, "there are rules. You all know them."

We shouted, "Fair game!"

Aaron faced the warriors, who stood ready to charge at each other.

"Simba, you're angry, right?"

"Angry like death!"

"So you want to destroy somebody, right?"

"To break some ribs!" Simba bore towards Ndudzo, but Aaron pushed him back.

"Ndudzo, you're angry, right?" Aaron asked.

"Like a mad lion!" Ndudzo said, as he attempted a roar.

"And you want to fight, you want to break something?"

"I want to bury him!" Ndudzo stamped his foot on the ground.

Aaron then turned to the crowd. "Everybody ready to enjoy a fight?"

"Ya-aaa!" we boomed. Cicada shrills from the girls, dull drones from the boys were heard. Aaron raised his fist to restore order. When we were silent, he scrapped together a mound of soil with his bare feet, smoothed it into a conical shape with his hand and turned to Ndudzo. "This is the breast of Simba's mother. Simba angered you and you want to teach him a lesson. Now kick his mother's breast." He moved out of the way. "Destroy it now, Ndudzo! Kick it like it's a piece of dung."

Ndudzo bounded forward and stopped, hesitated. The crowd groaned and cursed. Linda, Aaron's half-sister, shot forward and danced towards the breast. She swung her legs close to it. Then she challenged Ndudzo with a flash of her eyes, threatening to kick the breast. Ndudzo shook his head and stiffened. Linda bowed and danced back to the crowd. Ndudzo flew forward and kicked the mound of soil. There went Simba's mother's breast in a cloud of dust. We roared again, chanting Ndudzo's name.

Aaron formed another breast and told Simba to destroy it, to show that he still thought he could beat Ndudzo. Simba unleashed a kick that destroyed Ndudzo's mother's breast to nothing.

A-ah, this was it. We spread out to open more room for the fighters. Fists formed and teeth clenched. Legs danced and arms scooped air like an ally. Some in the crowd gestured in tune to the fighters' every movement. There was a palpable impatience in the air, as if the fight was taking too long to begin. We knew it was out of character for Simba to let a fight drag. A new strategy of his?

Ndudzo released swift blows that Simba received with laughter. Ndudzo stopped, breathing heavily, and Simba began dancing, then he slapped Ndudzo on the mouth, but Ndudzo threw a punch that caught his foe on the chin, causing him to stagger backwards. We clapped hands in earnest, and this marked the real beginning of the fight.

As Simba took the rapid punches, he looked just as surprised as we were. Fighting with Ndudzo, a boy his age, Simba was not supposed to do it, so we were more than shocked when he gave his famous roar, one that he usually gave when fighting someone older. We cheered for Ndudzo who had caused Simba to roar.

But in no time, Ndudzo was down, begging for mercy as Simba trampled on him. Simba stomped and told Ndudzo to clap his hands and shout that his mother was a witch.

"My mother is a witch!" shouted Ndudzo, clapping.

"King Simba, your father is the richest man in Mhototi," Simba said.

"King Simba, your father is the richest man on earth!" Ndudzo repeated after him.

"What else?" Simba stepped on Ndudzo's head.

"He is the most hardworking man in all of Mhototi. He didn't leave his job. It's the company that closed."

"What else?" Simba brought his foot close to Ndudzo's neck.

"You're the bull of Mhototi!" Ndudzo clapped and struggled to break free.

Simba kicked Ndudzo again and again and pinned him down harder. We were so immersed in applause for Simba that we did not notice the arrival of Teacher Mangena. But as soon as he started breaking through the ring, Aaron called for order, and the fighters rejoined the crowd.

"What's going on here, Aaron?" the teacher asked.

Aaron opened his mouth but he closed it immediately.

"Has some work been going on here?" The teacher's eyes scanned the crowd.

"We finished everything you told us to do," Aaron said, "and we were just waiting to be dismissed."

"So what was the noise about? We could hear it all the way from the staff room."

Aaron did not say anything; he looked confused.

Teacher Mangena turned his attention to the vegetable beds. He smiled and, looking at Aaron, said, "Now finish off your work and dismiss."

After the teacher left, Simba made Ndudzo apologise one more time, which he did, clapping.

For a whole week, everyone talked about this fight, praising Ndudzo for standing up against Simba. But we all knew that Simba was still the victor and most wouldn't dare cross him.

And here I had just told Mukoma I could beat Simba. The thought of fighting with him made me shudder, but I did not reveal this fear to Mukoma. It was one of my greatest days with Mukoma; I even enjoyed using my axe and feeling like a real man as I hacked into tree branches.

That Monday, I woke up early and went to Runde River for a cold bath. When Mukoma was at home, I washed at the river, even in June, when the water cut the skin like a knife. Mukoma was asleep when I left, but when I returned, I found him outside brushing his teeth. He spat and said, "Did you wash up thoroughly?"

"Yes," I said. "Good morning, Mukoma."

"You still look dirty," he said, walking away from me.

"I was running on my way back," I lied. "I don't want to be late for school."

"Wake up earlier next time. A real man should be a friend of water," he said, without turning to look at me.

I thanked him and then started preparing for school.

Maiguru had fried fat-cooks the night before, and I found her in the kitchen making tea. We drank tea when Mukoma was around, and for several weeks after he left for Harare. On such days, I was one of the few pupils who came to school having had tea. Simba's family, like many others in Mhototi, drank tea only at Christmas and, even then, the tea was usually plain, with no milk, no bread, and no white sugar to go with it. Mukoma always said as long as he worked, his family would drink tea the right way, with bread and butter, milk and white sugar. Brown sugar was for the poor, who couldn't afford to drink tea year-long.

After breakfast, I left for school, joining other chattering students. The morning was chilly, but some of us kicked a plastic and paper ball to stay warm, others jogged and skipped about. Our walk to school usually took thirty minutes. If we arrived late, we would find the teachers waiting for us with whips at the main entrance. But on this Monday we arrived on time.

I saw Simba in the crowd and kept my eyes on him. He turned his bald head and looked at me with a frown. My heart pounded, but I took a deep breath to calm down. I even looked away to continue with my business of going to school. When I turned again, just to check if he had looked away, I found him still staring in my direction. Then he started tearing his way towards me. Did he know something?

"Stop there, Fati," Simba said, trotting after me because I had broken into a jog. "Now!" he shouted. He was so close that I could hear his breathing.

His shout attracted a handful of students whose walking slackened. I was not jogging anymore, but I kept walking fast. I didn't want to be late, and Simba couldn't tell me to stop. He was not a teacher.

"You're playing with a python, Fati!" He spoke with a breathless voice. "Stop there, you useless pig!"

I turned and said, "Me? Stop? Why?"

"You know why," he said. "You know what you told your brother."

My heart started beating faster. "I don't know what you're talking about," I said.

He spat on the side of the road and sped up until he caught up with me. I walked faster, thrusting longer strides than his. He jumped in front of me and outstretched his arms to block me. I bent down to pass on his left side, but he swung his arms and I stopped. Fast as lightning, he poked my cheek with his coarse finger. I felt but ignored the pain as a hesitant sensation of anger began to seize me. Anger at Mukoma for causing this.

A group of boys whistled. I trembled and felt a stale taste in my mouth, the kind I always felt when Mukoma was about to beat me up. This is not the kind of attention I liked to get at school, to be known as another of Simba's victims. I was not the fighting type. I was not like Mukoma.

Simba stepped on my foot, pressed down, but I broke free and kept walking, ignoring the pain caused by his tire sandals. I knew I should show that I was getting upset, but that's not what I wanted Simba to see. His eyes were red, promising murder. Out of the corners of my eyes, I saw the crowd thickening around us like phantoms.

"This is the last time I'm going to tell you to stop," he said. "Blast me now, you donkey face!"

"I don't blast people," I said, walking faster. A trail of boys and girls pushed closer to us, some already jabbing the air with their fists. I looked straight ahead and pretended I was just walking to school as usual, with nothing out of the ordinary happening. I wanted to close my ears too, and to shut the shouts off, but each step I took was slower than the one before, as if I dreaded arriving at school. I would have paid anything for Simba to remember that I was a coward.

The crowd formed a wide ring around us, and I sensed mounting danger, but I wasn't going to fight with anyone; I was going to school and nothing would stop me. My body shook with what I hoped showed itself to Simba as fear. But he started to jump and kick like a bull testing its horns on the trunk of a tree. My chest tightened with fear.

"Do what you said you would do." He spoke in a low voice.

"I didn't say anything."

"Lying won't help you," he said. "Do it now." Then he looked at the crowd and shouted, "Hey people, I'm going to be blasted today!"

The crowd cheered, and someone shouted, "Be blasted then! Don't waste our time."

I moved closer to Simba and whispered, "We're friends and friends don't fight."

I felt a smile spreading across my face. Smiling often helped; the coward always smiled, hoping to be forgiven. It was a coward's dream to be judged harmless, innocent. I wanted to be innocent. If we were alone I would just kneel and beg for mercy, calling him "the bull", even though I believed that title only belonged to Mukoma. Even now, in front of these people, I wanted to shake Simba's hand, to show him what I had told Mukoma didn't mean anything. Only he and I knew what I had told Mukoma, so I didn't want him to involve all these people. We could talk about this in our village, I could apologise.

I leaned closer to him and whispered, "Hey."

"What?" he said.

"When Mukoma goes back to Harare he will leave me some money. I'll share it with you," I said.

He shook his head and jumped backwards. "No one needs your stupid money." He then unleashed a slap that stung my left cheek and sent a searing wave of pain to my eye. "That's just to wake you up," he said, offering his cheek for me to slap. There was no way I would do such a thing.

64

I touched my smarting cheek, forced a smile. A second slap landed on my other cheek, and as the pain chewed its way through my flesh, I heard loud laughter; and I couldn't decide then what pain I feared most, that of the slap or of the laughing crowd. I had watched Simba's fight the previous week and had been part of a laughing crowd, but I didn't want the same to happen to me. I hated this crowd.

Simba was raging, skipping about in provocation, sadly wasting his time because I wasn't going to fight him. If only the ground could open, it would swallow us both, and down under we would talk it over and reason with each other like men.

"Talk, little girl!" Simba said, prodding my ribs with his fist.

I don't know what got into me, but suddenly I wasn't afraid. I advanced towards him, and he seemed to shrink. I wanted to smash him. As the noise increased, I raised my fist to strike, but I lowered it again. No, I couldn't fight. I didn't want to make the same mistake Ndudzo had made last week. The look on Simba's face frightened me, more so because he wasn't acting surprised by my advance.

I was ready to kneel down and tell Simba he was the bull of Mhototi, meaning it this time. I leaned forward, amid loud cheering, and said, "Simba, please, let's reason together. We must not fight…" I stopped when Ndudzo shot from the crowd and stood beside Simba. I thought Ndudzo was coming to my rescue, so I moved closer and heard him say, "Don't listen to him."

"What do you want?" Simba said.

"Show him who the boss is," said Ndudzo.

"And why do you care? Because I thrashed you last week and now…?"

"Oh no; you have all the reasons to beat up this idiot," Ndudzo said. "Now the word spreading in all of Mhototi is how your family only drinks tea once a year. And guess who spread that," he paused and sighed, then pointed at me, "this one here."

Simba turned to face Ndudzo directly, "Don't play with me now."

"So how do you think I know that you use sacks as your blankets when you sleep?"

I started shaking. "Ndudzo, stop telling lies," I said.

"Just telling him what you told us at Runde River yesterday," Ndudzo said, and before I could set the record straight, he walked back into the crowd. Yes, I had said something close to that, but I had spoken it in confidence, something which wasn't supposed to reach Simba's ears, something which wasn't relevant to this moment; I had said Simba's family rarely drank tea, which was true, but again not relevant to the moment now. I hated Ndudzo.

Simba made as if to charge after Ndudzo, but the crowd booed him, and he swung around and grabbed my hand, and with his teeth clenched, told me to explain what Ndudzo had just said. I hesitated. I didn't know what to say, or what not to say. I preferred not to talk about any talks I had had with Ndudzo and others at the river.

The crowd surged forward. I was still trying to free myself from Simba's grip. Soon, the school bell would ring, and I didn't want to be late.

I jerked my hand backwards and freed myself from Simba's grip. With the same hand I pushed him and, to my surprise, he staggered backwards. The crowd roared. I thrust forward, trying to break through the ring to safety, but the chain of hands tightened. Simba sneered and planted himself in front of me. "Beat me now!" He followed up his words with a slap so hard my ears rang. I ducked to one side to avoid another slap, but it caught me on my nose, causing a thick yellow glob to squirt out of my nostrils. I felt the sting of another slap, then another, and another.

I didn't like that, no, no, no.

I felt my face throbbing. My right hand was shaking.

"Now you're getting angry?" Simba said. "Go ahead, hit me." He offered his face for me to hit, but I ignored him. He kicked my shin, and then he pushed me, waited, and pushed again.

A tight knot formed in my throat, everything shrunk, and I groaned...*then I saw Mukoma charging at Tukano.*

"He's attacking. Look!"

Mukoma's fist grazed Tukano's cheek. Tukano reeled backwards and banged against the bar counter.

Loud cheering erupted from the crowd as Simba struggled back to his feet, wiping his cheek. My knuckles burned.

"You dare beat me, coward?" shouted Simba. He jumped forward and sent a kick. *Mukoma dodged Tukano's kick and it landed on the counter, making him shriek with pain. Mukoma then jumped, made a wheel's reel and gave Tukano a donkey kick on the chest. Tukano fell down, bellowing with pain.*

"Fati! Fati!" I jumped from spot to spot, waiting for Simba, who struggled up again and bore forward, baring his bloodied teeth. His punch caught me on the eye, and I felt a burn. He jumped backwards, and then danced towards me, ready to release another blow. *Mukoma dashed backwards, calculating Tukano's angle of attack. He then rained crunching blows on Tukano's face — cha, cha, cha[5]— until blood gushed out. He kicked him on the groin and Tukano doubled over in pain. Mukoma jumped and spun like a screw. His feet landed on Tukano's stomach.*

Simba fell to the ground...and I wanted to take off running before he got up.

Everyone shouted my name. I stood in the middle of the crowd, unsure if I should jump in victory or just resume walking to school. Part of the crowd had left since the bell had rung. I was going to be late; Simba had made me late to school. I kicked him in the stomach and he rolled over on the ground. I kicked him again and again. It felt good to kick him; so I kicked some more, coughed out a laugh, kicked

---

5   *cha, cha, cha* - these are anomatopeic sounds imitating the sounds of blows on the
        victim.

again. And now I didn't care I was going to be late to school: I was already late. I better kick Simba some more then, so I kicked and kicked.

Suddenly, the crowd stopped shouting. Before I could turn to see why, a big hand grabbed my shoulder and pulled me back. I tilted my head backwards, looking up, and my eyes met those of Teacher Mangena, who said, "Is this you, Fati?"

"He started it," I said. "I didn't want to fight."

Simba jumped up and advanced towards me, poised to strike, but the teacher stopped him.

"So all this time you're the brute?" Teacher Mangena said.

"I didn't fight with him," I said, trembling. "He just fell."

The teacher looked around and lowered his head. In a whisper he said, "You did well." Then, audibly, he said, "You two are in big trouble. You know fighting is not allowed on school grounds." He then scanned the other students with his eyes. "And you, all of you, run to assembly before you upset me. Go!" They dispersed immediately. "You two, come with me to my office."

Simba and I followed Teacher Mangena. The way he walked in front of us, his limp less pronounced, walking like he owned the ground upon which we were walking, showed me, and perhaps Simba too, that we were in serious trouble, maybe some heavy caning or a referral to the headmaster's office afterwards, or both.

I looked at Simba and he returned my gaze. He cleared his throat and greeted me with a blood-smeared smile. I smiled back with my swollen lips. Maybe he was thinking what I was thinking, that soon after we entered Mangena's office, we would shake hands as friends do and apologise to each other. Teacher Mangena might still flog us, maybe reduce the number of stripes, and he might end up not sending us to the headmaster's office. To me, whatever awaited us in the teacher's office didn't matter more than the fact that Simba was now smiling. Any moment, I might be overpowered by the laughter that was building within me.

To the Gathering

On any other day, I would have used a stick chewed up on one end to brush my teeth, but this was an important event, so I used one of the many toothbrushes that had once belonged to my late brother, Edward. I squeezed the last smudge of toothpaste; something Maiguru would punish me for if she found out I did it. But I didn't care anymore about what she was going to do. I was going to that gathering and nothing — not even the duty to herd the goats, or other chores at home could stop me. The only person who could stop me, Mukoma, was away in South Africa and no one knew when he would return. I was to meet my friend Chari behind Chisiya Hill; then we would join the others walking to Mhototi Primary School. We would arrive before the service began.

I wore a black pair of trousers, a long-sleeved grey shirt, and my one pair of shoes, which shone in the sunlight and showed my reflection when I looked at them. I had ironed my shirt nicely, creating creases sharp enough to slice a fly. I looked good, way better than Chari would look, although he had said he would surprise me. But what he called surprises always turned out to be cheap imitations of my style. He didn't have a sense of fashion.

I looked at my face in a small mirror on my Afro-comb and saw the smile that would dazzle those Mberengwa girls, but I wasn't going there for the girls. I just had to arrive on time, to get there before other teams arrived. Satisfied, a small notebook in hand, I started my careful walk towards Chisiya Hill. As I reached the edge of the compound, with its crown of leaning grass, I heard the urgent sound of Maiguru MaMoyo's footsteps. She was staggering under the weight of a big water bucket. The look on her face showed that she disapproved of what I was about to do. She hurried into the kitchen hut to set the bucket down. In no time, she shot out and looked at me with a hard face, her hands resting on her waist, her head tilted to one side. If she thought she could stop me she was fooling herself.

I resumed walking and pretended that she was not there. A warm feeling of freedom flowed through my body, and my mind focused on what lay ahead. People at the gathering were going to see the real me, no more silly shyness, no hesitation in conversation. I would be the one to initiate dialogue with the guests from Mberengwa; I wanted them to leave Mhototi with a clear picture of who I was. Chari wanted to be noticed too; in fact, he had the idea that only he would stand out from the youths of Mhototi and had already said he thought the people of Mberengwa would make him the leader of our new group, but he just didn't know how I would surprise him.

I increased my speed, still careful not to make my shoes dirty.

"Where do you think you are going?" Maiguru said, her voice relaxed. She seemed to think that stopping me would be easy. Maybe ten months ago that would have been true, but not now. I slowed down though, turned and said, "I told you this morning where I'm going."

"And where're you going?"

"You already know."

"But you can't go to the pastures in those clothes. You look like someone going to church," she said. "If your brother hears you abuse the clothes he toils for in South Africa, he will kill you dead."

"No, he won't!" I said.

"You think so?" She coughed out a laugh. "Wait until he returns. You know what the tall, dark man can do."

"If he returns," I corrected her. Her face darkened suddenly, and I felt like I had scored a point. I knew she feared that Mukoma might not return, and I wanted her to understand that her threat would not work anymore.

She started walking towards me, slowly, like she had no reason to be in a hurry. Maybe she didn't have to be, but to give her a reason, I resumed walking vigorously.

"Hey! Did you hear what I said? You can't go to the goats like that!"

"You know I'm going to no goats," I said, getting a little upset at myself for allowing her to keep talking to me like this. "You know where I'm going. You knew this morning, you knew yesterday."

"Oh, so you are actually going somewhere?" She paused. She might even have stopped walking. "And where're you going again, exactly?"

I wasn't going to answer that. If she thought I was playing games with her, she was wrong, just as she had been wrong about many things. Wasn't she the one who had told me that Mukoma would return in two months, and then two months turned to five, then two years?

"Answer me!" she said, raising her voice. "Where do you think you're going?"

I pointed in the direction of Mhototi Primary School and continued walking.

"Are you going to the *gungano*?"[1] she asked with a tone of urgency.

She was right, and I confirmed this by walking faster.

"Because, if you are," she paused, as if she had forgotten what to say next, "you are not."

I knew it! she knew. I walked without worrying about anything and started whistling a tune, one of the new songs I had learned the day before, a song for the gathering. Were it not for my shoes I would have danced my way to the school; it was important to keep them shiny until I arrived at the gathering. Of course, they would become dirty once I started dancing, but I hoped everyone would have seen me by then. It was very important, that and the need to arrive early, to get time to talk with the visitors. I was going to have to force myself to talk with them, to present myself as a confident, groomed youth.

"Hey you! I'm not going to let you go to those strange people."

Ah, so she was still following me. I turned and said, "Listen, I'm going." I started walking in reverse. "And who told you those people are strange?"

---

1   *gungano* - a big church gathering

Maiguru laughed scornfully, then the laughter died suddenly, but its ghost lingered on her face. I could see it turning into anger; a deep honest anger meant to scare me, but sorry, not today.

I could already picture the crowd under the huge *muvunga* tree at the primary school where *Varanda Vashe*,[2] the Mberengwa people she was calling strange, had rented several classrooms for the weekend. They had brought many girls, and for beauty to be concentrated in a single group like that was almost a sin, but I didn't look bad either. Chari was alright too, but everyone would see that I was the centre of focus, but not if Chari, Ngoni and others arrived before I did; I couldn't let that happen.

"Come back here, boy!" Maiguru shouted, speeding towards me.

"You don't call me boy!" I said, my lips shaking.

Although I was only fourteen, she had no right to call me boy. As my big brother's wife, she was only supposed to call me *babamunini*.[3] If Mukoma ever found out that she called me boy, he would make her wish she had never been born. If anyone was likely to be beaten by Mukoma for anything, she was the one, not me. I wasn't afraid of anything; I knew Mukoma would not beat me up for not listening to her. Before he left, he had said, "You are a big man now. Take care of things. Protect your Maiguru." He had even told me once that when he was away, I was the man of the house, helping with chores, and listening, which I also took to mean being listened to. Even Mai had told me to stand my ground if Maiguru ever tried to beat me again, as she had done when I was nine. Mother even went on to say, "She's as good as your wife. If your brother dies, you could easily become her real husband when you grow up."

I stiffened and started walking tall; legs wide apart like a giant's.

---

2   *Varanda Vashe* - humble servants of the Lord (is also the name of the church)
3   *babamunini* - a title of respect for the husband's younger brother to the speaker.

"You're surely asking for a beating today, silly boy," she said, breaking into a jog after me, which made her look like a locust with broken wings.

"I'm going to the gathering!" I shouted.

"No, you are not." She continued to jog, breathing in gasps.

"I really am!" I broke into a trot too, but I didn't want her to think that I was running away from her, so I slowed down to a walk.

"Keep thinking you're going and you'll see what I do to you," she said. I could sense the false victory of her anger. She had a way to show anger with a laughing voice which I never understood, but which had frequently scared me.

"Yes, what can you do?" I asked, stopping.

"Have you ever been beaten like a snake that has entered someone's hut?" I could hear her heavy breathing. "Come back here right now."

She was wasting my time. I walked faster.

"Don't think because you're now tall that you can do what you want here." She cleared her throat. "You're still a child."

No I'm not, I thought, resisting the urge to turn, but the skin on my back crawled the way it did when a whip was about to land on it. I had no reason to fear her now. That was out of the question.

"If I say don't go, then you're not going. It's that simple," she said. She caught up with me and overtook me; then, walking in reverse, she tried to block my way by spreading her arms sideways, but she just managed to look like someone nailed on a cross. She leaned forward and said, "Go back home and take off those clothes. Now!"

As I tried to pass by her left side, she swung and blocked me. "I'm going to kill you." She pointed at me with a shaking finger. Her expression was dry, suggesting extreme anger. For a moment, I felt like cringing, but no, not today. "Don't play with me boy, understand?" she said.

Coming from Mukoma, the word 'understand' would have carried much weight, but coming from her…no, I wasn't going to understand anything.

I jumped to the right edge of the path, landing too close to a thorn bush, but there she was again, her outstretched arms flailing. "You're not going to that church of evil!" She was drenched in sweat. "Evil people are not good for anyone in Mhototi." She kept doing her funny dance of trying to block me. Everything about her was dancing, her chest, the torn blouse she wore, and her oversized brown skirt that looked like a sack. "I say no to evil, and you should too."

She didn't know me that well. She was used to the bed-wetting boy she had always beaten with a raw-hide whip, then bribed with sweets when Mukoma was close to returning home for the holidays. Back, when he worked in Harare, back when he used to bring us white sugar for our tea. Now she couldn't trick me in any way. I was old enough to defend myself. I would do it better than Chari had done to his *maiguru* only two weeks ago. His Maiguru had tried to beat him up for forgetting to close the chicken run the night before, but he had stood his ground, reminding her that he was a grown-up man. She had thought he would run away when she took out his brother's belt, but Chari had snatched the belt from her hand and struck her twice before he took off running to tell me about it. He had felt good, and he would do it again if she disrepected him. I had laughed at him for running away, but he told me he remembered his brother may have been somewhere near. Although his brother came home later and beat him up, Chari still bragged to me that he had changed the way his *maiguru* treated him. I was going to do better.

"Get out of my way!" I said, then lowering my voice, added, "please." She extended her arm to push me backwards. I dodged and lost my balance and fell on the side of the road. I sprung up, my cheeks throbbing with anger, and charged towards her, thinking if she chose not to move out of my way, she might as well be prepared to fall like a *mutsviri* tree struck by lightning, but she stiffened and laughed as if my efforts were funny. For a moment, I felt funny too. I stopped right in front of her, my eyes fixed on hers. Still, she didn't move. She even gave a stupid smile.

I had no time for this. Chari was waiting for me behind Chisiya, looking forward to seeing my new dance moves at the gathering. I didn't want him to leave without me, nor did I want to miss the first dance session, which would feature the youths from Mberengwa. Just the thought of their lead singer's voice tearing the air and the first drum wailing in response made me want to do something, I didn't know what, to Maiguru. Anything at all for her to leave me alone. But she started charging towards me again, poised to push.

I turned around sharply and ran back to the compound. First, I looked on the ground in front of the kitchen hut, but I had no idea what I was looking for. I thought of entering the kitchen to get a knife, but that made me feel like I was a murderer, so I looked under the stilts of the granary instead. I wanted to teach her a lesson; I wanted to stop her from stopping me from going. I found nothing under the granary. I proceeded to the storage hut, kicked the door open and grabbed the first tool I saw, a long, metal rod we used to dig pole holes. I hoped that she would have moved out of the path by the time I re-emerged, but she was still standing on the same spot, her hands on her waist. She was grinning even, looking at me like I didn't exist.

I tore my way straight towards her, and as I drew closer, she seemed to be shrinking. I was going to kill her. There was nothing more important than the promise I had made to Chari. The dance moves I had practised for a whole week, which I was going to surprise the congregation with; no one could stop me from going to show them off. There would be people applauding there at Mhototi, people wondering who I was, asking each other, "Who is he?" while others proudly claimed me as their friend, nephew, or cousin, or brother. The people would call my name, they would beg for more moves. I couldn't miss all that for anything. Besides, this was going to be the launch of our branch of the new church. I didn't want to miss the opportunity of being considered a possible youth leader by the end of the service and the launch. And if no adult would be converted yet, there was a chance that I might even be made a deacon, or some kind of leader for the Mhototi branch.

I drew dangerously closer to Maiguru and raised the rod, but I wasn't sure yet if I was going to strike. I hoped she would get out of the way, but she did not. She just opened her eyes wider and ducked backwards.

"What do you think you're doing, boy?" she said. "Just try any silliness and I will beat you until you die." She stamped the ground with her bare feet. "Like this — see? — until you die!"

I raised the rod and leapt forward to strike, but instead of running she burst out laughing, doubling over and choking on her laughter. I remained frozen, metal rod raised. Then when she collapsed again with laughter, like nothing dangerous was about to happen, I started lowering the metal towards her head. This time I was going to whack her. She must have seen my seriousness because she stopped laughing, turned around and took off towards Chigorira Hill. At first, she seemed to run on the same spot, so I let her cover some distance; planning to run after her a little later. Once I caught up with her, I would whack her like a baboon that has stolen maize from someone's field.

She had already delayed me. I would miss the first round of the dancing, the one where the Mberengwa girls would spring to their feet, form into two lines, as the circle of people around them widened to give them more room, and plough the earth with their bare feet. They would quiver to one side, then sway and hammer the ground in tune to the deep groans of the bass drums and the tremor of the tenor. I didn't want to miss the part they would spread out and not even pay attention to their flying skirts as their bodies shot high into the air and hit the ground like hail, only to bounce up again like their feet were made out of springs. The crowd always went wild, clapping and ululating, drowning the drums with their singing...

I chased her. She ran faster than I had ever imagined her capable of, even though she leaned to the left side as she ran. The thrill of it, the fact that the person who had once chased me across the village was the

76

one running away from me made my heart flutter with excitement. And if she thought that I would give up pursuing her, she was dreaming. I was right behind her now.

"You're crazy!" she shouted without turning or slowing down.

Her feet raised a cloud of dust that chased her faster than I was. She kept running, without turning or shouting anything, which showed me that I had won, that she was afraid of me, but I wasn't done with her. We ran past Chimombe's home, where, fortunately, no one was at home, and as I scanned other homes around us, I didn't see anyone looking at us. I wouldn't have wanted anyone to see me doing this.

When we reached Chigorira, there was nowhere for her to run to. She could stop and face me, perhaps try to attack me, in which case I would run towards Chisiya, then once there, I would chase her again, or she could start climbing the steep, slippery rocks. She chose to climb, but made a serious mistake; she jumped onto a rock and slipped. What happened next brought me to a standstill.

She fell and landed on the bare ground with her back. My eyes met hers, which opened widely like those of a doll. I dropped the rod, turned and ran away in the direction of Runde River. After running for a while, I hid behind a dense, thorn bush. I wanted to peek and see if she was still alive, if she was going to get up. I couldn't see her clearly through the matted branches. I leaned closer, but thorns grabbed my shirt. I was almost done untangling myself when I heard some shuffling behind me, and before I could turn to look, my pants, together with the underwear, were suddenly pulled down. I wrenched myself free from the thorns and turned around. Maiguru stood in front of me swaying with laughter. I covered my private parts with my hands, turned around again. There was nowhere in the bush to hide, nowhere to run away since she blocked the only way I could have escaped by.

"Too late, little husband," Maiguru said with a hoarse voice. "You think you're a man, prove it now."

"What are you talking about?" I said, turning on time to see her leaning forward and lifting her skirt. "No, please, no!" I said, pressing into the bush, feeling thorns clawing on my back.

"You're a man now, little husband, right?" Maiguru said, licking her lips.

"No, I didn't say that!"

"You didn't say what?" I could feel her warm breath on my ear.

"I'm not your...husband," I said.

My heart felt as if it was going to escape from my chest. I wanted to run away from this crazy woman. She extended her arms, grabbed my waist, and I struggled. She pulled me towards her with a power I didn't know she possessed, groaning, and laughing like a witch, but I held on to a branch of the thorn bush; then I felt her hand on my thigh, closer and closer to where my hand covered my stiffening nakedness. "No, please, no!" I said, kicking and wrenching myself free from her grip and before she realised it I turned and pushed her into the bush, pulled my pants up and flew in the direction of Mai's home.

I ran for a while without turning, and when Mai's home came into view, I changed my direction. I still wanted to go to the gathering, so I ran in the direction of Mhototi road. I kept running, my head swimming, my heart pounding. It was an indescribable feeling that kept me running, and I did not want to think about or believe what had just happened. I ran and ran towards Chisiya, past Rombe's home, thinking about how I was not going to tell Chari what had just happened. I was gripped by a sense of urgency, convinced that Chari had already left without me. Then I heard a twig break in the thicket on the left side of the path and I slowed down. I heard Mai's voice, saying, "Where are you running to like that, boy?" Then she emerged from the thicket, carrying a bundle of firewood.

I broke into a run again without answering her. I could sense that my mother was still looking at me.

"Where do you think you are going?" she shouted after me, and I slowed down and said, "Nowhere, just running!"

"Liar!" she said. "Just say you are off to that dancing church of yours. Make sure you don't spend all night there. You have to help your Maiguru with the chores. You are the man of the house now, understand?"

I increased my speed, running away from her words and their man-of-the-house message. Nothing, not even Mai, nor Maiguru, not even Mukoma, would stop me from going to that gathering. After a while of running, I felt lighter, as if I had been freed from some heavy sins. I did not bother to check for Chari behind the hill. I wanted to continue running without thinking about Maiguru, but whenever I tried to forget about her, I kept seeing the smile on her face when she had leaned closer to me, saying, "Let's see you be a man, little husband." I could not forget the fall, and the craziness I had seen in her eyes, then the huskiness of her voice behind the thorn bush when she said, "Yes, now, now, little husband." I wanted to arrive at the gathering as soon as possible. In my mind's eye, I saw people dancing in a big circle, round and round, non-stop…

As I reached the main road, I saw a group of boys and girls walking towards me. I slowed down to capture a better view. As they drew closer, I saw Chari and Ngoni in front. They seemed to be arguing about something, but I soon noticed that they were laughing. They started running towards me and I came to a complete stop, confused. Shouldn't they be walking towards the school? Was the gathering over already? Had they decided not to go after I failed to show up?

"You should thank evil spirits," Chari shouted, "for causing the service to be cancelled."

Then he turned to Ngoni who nodded in confirmation.

Service cancelled? How was that possible? I moved to the side of the road, to get out of their way since they were still walking fast. But they slowed down, and all faces turned to me.

"I was going to show you your little dance moves are nothing; then I was going to have the whole school laugh at you tomorrow," Chari said, as he signalled the group of four boys and five girls to stop in front of me in a semi-circle. They all looked at me weirdly.

I didn't say anything, my mind racing: the running after Maiguru, the look in her eyes after she fell from the rock, her hands on my waist, the stir in my groin… but why had the service been cancelled?

"One of the deacons fell and hurt himself badly," said Chari as if he had read my mind. "The elders had to take him…" he turned to Ngoni. "Where did they take him?"

"To Gudo," said Ngoni, waving dismissively in the direction of Gudo Village.

The others stood like disciples of Chari and Ngoni, stupid grins on their faces. They looked at me like I was naked…and the girls; it was as if they could smell what had happened between me and Maiguru. What had she been trying to do, moving closer like she was crazy?

"Look at him," said Chari, "standing there like an idiot." He squinted his eyes at me as if he too was beginning to see on my face what had delayed me. I didn't want him to see anything, so I looked away. "Hey, what happened to that?" he asked.

"What?" I said, slowly looking between my legs.

"Your shirt sleeve, it's chewed up," he said.

"Oh, I fell while trying to be on time," I said.

They burst out laughing. Chari said, "Anyway, my boy, now you have to come with us to something more interesting."

"What's that?" I said, fighting an image of the falling Maiguru.

"Follow first, find out later," he said, signalling the group to resume walking. "Come on, let's go, but you're overdressed."

"That's okay," said Ngoni. "At least we will have one weirdo among us."

They laughed again as they resumed walking with their faces still turned to me. A group of walking boys and girls returning from a disrupted gathering, but already going somewhere more interesting, could not be ignored. I too started walking towards wherever they were going, even felt a new surge of joy as I thought of what awaited me there, but I slowed down to stay at the back of the group, away from Chari and Ngoni who were talking too much.

When we reached Chisiya again, I glanced in the direction of our home, and my heart skipped a beat when I saw Mai and Maiguru walking towards Mhototi Primary School. They were not talking, but their urgency was unmistakable. They hadn't seen me yet, so I sunk deeper into the group and focused my thinking on what lay ahead.

The Big Day

By the time Brutus stabbed me, Mukoma had already left to fight with the Mhere boys. Earlier in the morning, at home, he had told me that he just wanted to come and hear my English, and to see if I had the right gestures for it, adding that he was not interested in the prize-winning ceremony that would follow the big performance, nor did he care about meeting with my teachers to discuss my progress. I don't think when he left I had finished dying because even before Mark Anthony arrived at the scene, half the audience had left the play and had gone to watch Mukoma's fight. Miss Mukaro, the teacher who had directed the performance, came to where I lay dead and whispered, "Caesar, your big brother." I sprang up and looked where Mukoma had been standing and saw that he was gone. Then I saw four men running towards the back of the school and soon, my wounds still oozing blood, I was chasing them.

I caught up with the men, who didn't even notice me, but I could tell by the way they wrung their hands, how they formed fists and jabbed the air, that they were excited about the fight. They yelled as if this fight alone was the most important thing in their lives, as if it was more interesting than our performance. I sped up and overtook them. I couldn't run with idiots who did not know what was important to me, to all the students, to the teachers, to Mhototi, to all of Zimbabwe. I wanted to arrive at the fight before too many people. I wanted to distract Mukoma, to do anything that would allow us to finish the performance, for Anthony to bury Caesar. But even as I sprinted towards the scene, I realised that my presence would not stop any fight, that, if anything, the fight might worsen. I ran anyway, now feeling the weight of my costume and the dull brushing sound of its plastic legs as I ran. The blood, too, was still pouring out; I was now wasting it before all of Brutus's people had washed their hands and swords in it.

I stopped running and started walking slowly. I didn't want to go to the fight anymore, so I leaned against a tree on the edge of the school yard and watched people rushing by. Most didn't see me, and those who did just smiled and continued running. I wanted to return to the huge *muvunga* tree where the stage of our play was, but I also wanted to see how Mukoma was doing, to see how his opponents were doing. Maybe he would see me in my costume and the fake blood from the stabs of Brutus and his thugs. This might distract him for sure. I knew he had missed the stabbing part, and he might for a moment think I was injured.

A restless crowd had gathered around the tall gum tree behind the PE building. People were struggling to get to the front; they shouted and shoved, and side fights might start soon. What was wrong with these people? Adults who were supposed to be at the *muvunga* tree watching the performance were here acting like children. What was Mhototi coming to? Just seeing them made my blood boil. What was Mukoma doing, embarrassing me like this, blocking all the chances I had to receive the help Miss Mukaro had promised?

I started shaking with anger, but I approached the scene carefully. I didn't want to be seen by anyone who knew Mukoma as my brother. I pushed forward, but my way was blocked by some youth leaders singing war songs from the Chimurenga, the war Mukoma had despised and avoided, so he always fought with men who had been in it. I could tell that the singing men supported the Mhere boys; there was no way they could be on Mukoma's side and sing about the war in the same breath. Besides, they seemed intent on blocking me from seeing the fighters. Mukoma must have been doing well; otherwise they would not try to stop me. With the youth leaders' support, the Mhere boys were not likely to surrender soon. Since Mukoma was not known for surrendering as well, this was going to be a long fight. Now I wanted to see Mukoma thrashing the Mhere brothers really good, like he had done on many occasions. Mukoma's fights happened so frequently that sometimes I wondered how he escaped death, but he had told me that he would die once I was done with school.

If Mukoma ended up winning this fight like he always did, I would be popular among my schoolmates. I even saw my classmates, Ngoni and Tari, jumping up and down, taking turns to climb on each other's shoulders to get a better view. They took turns to climb down and twist with joy, punching the air with fists and clapping hands for Mukoma, no doubt. I could not let them see me, so I tiptoed to the other side of the crowd. I heard what I always heard when Mukoma was fighting: "*Chibhakera icho! Gidi!*"[1] I didn't know what this meant, but I guessed it had to do with fists that were like powerful guns. A man freed himself from the crowd, twisted his body, clapped, and said, "That's what I call fighting." He then forced his way back, pushing away a man who had taken his spot. I didn't know whether I should be proud or disappointed, but there was no mistaking the fact that these people were enjoying the fight. I was used to Mukoma being popular for his fights in Mhototi, but I had never thought he would bring his fights to school. Some of the people here may not have guessed who was going to win, but I had watched too many of Mukoma's fights to know.

The Mhere boys, like most of Mukoma's rivals, hated that he had not gone to the war of liberation, and that he was now enjoying the fruits of independence, which, in my view, included two droughts so far and, therefore, government or donor-grain handouts to the village, and subsidised education for all students. As his younger brother, if I was to continue enjoying the benefits of free government education, people like the Mhere boys wanted Mukoma to prove that he had contributed to the war and demands on Mukoma always led to fights. Besides, he always told them that his life in South Africa had been a kind of war, and having survived Soweto, he could survive anything in Mhototi. Not even those who had squeezed the trigger of a gun could pose a threat to him. Most men feared him, yet the Mhere boys, whose former girlfriend Mukoma had married, were his persistent rivals, all

---

1   *Chibhakera icho! Gidi!* - a thunderous fist hitting a victim

84

four of them, who had taken turns to fall in and out of love with the same woman, that same woman still sitting back at the *muvunga* tree because she was Mukoma's wife—had been for seven years — and because she hated watching Mukoma fight, especially with the Mhere boys, whose insistence on fighting for her like the world had no other women, she resented.

Finally, I broke through a fence of girls and the fighters came into view. I couldn't believe what I saw. Mukoma and his friend Jakove were murdering the Mhere boys, two against four. I hadn't expected to see Jakove; I didn't even know if he would be in Mhototi this weekend, let alone at the school open house, since he didn't have children. I felt a wave of joy when I realised that he had come to support me as Mukoma had, but now, if I chose, I could support them in their impromptu drama, but I didn't like its timing.

They stood back to back, each handling two of the boys, who bulldozed into them, only to be punched and kicked back to the ground. The boys would struggle up, groaning, wiping blood with their palms and advance again, panting like dogs, shouting "*Bathakathi!*",[2] which either meant witches or wizards, but Mukoma and Jakove stood like granite boulders. For a moment, I forgot I was angry at Mukoma. Seeing their act made me smile.

Someone in the crowd shouted, "Fists of Egoli! Fists of Wenela!" These were names by which people called Mukoma and Jakove, referring to South Africa, where both men had spent five years each. Since they had worked in gold mines, and didn't have much to show for it, people believed the experience had at least given them fists of gold, which I thought of as fists of granite, because they demolished rather than ornamented what they came in contact with. But the Mhere boys of Chimurenga fists would fight until they were covered in blood and would surrender only when they had just enough breath left to challenge Mukoma to the next fight.

---

2   *Bathakhathi* - a Ndebele term for witches or wizards

The men fought, the Mhere boys panting and toiling while Jakove and Mukoma released blows and kicks with ease, every now and then turning to check how the other was doing, which was just a way to show that they wanted the fight to go on since the crowd had grown denser and it seemed no one was thinking about our performance anymore. No one was looking at me and my Roman costume.

I looked away from the fighters and scanned the crowd for other costumes from my cast, the *dramatis personae*, as we had been taught to call ourselves. I saw Cassius, still in his costume, standing near Portia, leaning forward and clamouring to get a better view. I started to look for Mark Anthony, who by now had forgotten about exiting the stage with my body, but I did not see him. Instead, I saw Brutus standing behind my fresh widow, Calpurnia. It was possible that the whole cast was here, perhaps resenting me for being related to Mukoma. Brutus started to clap vigorously. I looked at the fighters and saw that Jakove was down and his two Mhere foes were stomping on him. But soon, he was up, jumping and kicking them to the ground. Brutus' arms fell to his sides. I jumped, punching my fist in the air, but stopped when my eyes met Mukoma's. He frowned and quickly returned his attention to the fight.

While he wanted me to have his courage, he always told me that there was a time for everything, that I had to focus on school for now, and maybe later I would have my reasons to fight with the world. I sank deeper into the crowd and began to think about what my teacher would say, how other teachers were going to treat me when they discovered that my brother was involved in the disruption of the programme. I knew it was the Mhere boys' fault. Why had they shown up at the school on a day clearly labelled 'Parents Day'? Yes, Mukoma and Jakove were not parents yet, but Mukoma, eighteen years older than me, was like my father. He was entitled to come to the school as a parent and watch his son proving that he was the best speaker of English.

The boys, grown-up men as tall as Jakove and Mukoma, did everything together, like one person. Some said, as little boys, they had helped their mother in the kitchen, since they had no sister, so their boyhood stood out. The villagers stopped using their names altogether and just called them the Mhere boys; and indeed, they were known for causing trouble as their name implied. They had terrorised the village immediately after the war in 1980, forcing everyone to go to nightly party meetings. Granted, we all liked the dancing, we all liked the singing — there were contests which helped some raise a little money — but the beatings of party enemies in 1982 made the Mhere boys unpopular. They would beat you up for being late or for disrupting the meeting, which all were worthy causes, but the number of lashes they gave went beyond the rules of common decency. Because they were the Mhere boys, youth leaders, ex-combatants, strong industrious young men, the villagers allowed them to do as they wished.

When Mukoma returned from South Africa, immediately followed by Jakove, who asked for a piece of land to build his home in the nearby village of Chakavanda where he had found a woman to marry, the Mhere boys had found their match! Mukoma told them that if they were real men, they should stop the party beatings and fight him at every meeting, to which they agreed, requesting that Jakove join Mukoma so they would feel like they were fighting with a man, by which they implied that fighting either Mukoma or Jakove alone would be like fighting a woman. This enraged Mukoma who beat them up that night of the first challenge. Round one. Then on the very next day they arrived at our home carrying spears and knobkerries and Mukoma surrendered first, and they told him they wanted to fight again and that they would not use the weapons, which they agreed to put in a heap at the edge of our compound. They fought with Mukoma for a whole hour. One by one, when they were all bleeding they surrendered. They agreed that it had been a fair fight, everyone was injured, everyone was bleeding.

As they were leaving, they told Mukoma that this was just the beginning and he reminded them that it was the second match, but if they wanted to count it the first, that was fine with him. They nodded their swollen heads and confirmed that they counted it the first. Round one again. All the subsequent fights would be counted firsts, so in fighting with the Mhere boys, Jakove and Mukoma were always in round one, and they didn't mind it at all.

So this, too, was round one, happening where it was not supposed to, yet, with the presence of Jakove, looking as planned as the previous ones. The way they formed into two neat teams, as if they had rehearsed this, and the boys' blood, a spectacle deeper than the brooding wounds of my costume, whose blood had begun to dry up. The costumes had been the idea of the science teacher, a British expatriate who was studying the thorn bushes of my village. She had specially ordered the costumes from the British Council in Harare, and had explained to us that the idea would thrill the villagers, who had never seen these kinds of costumes before, and that the simulated blood would make some think that I had been stabbed for real. And yes, I had heard the gasps and grunts of some of the audience members, but shortly after this fight had begun, attracting the curiosity of the audience more than my sprawling on the ground, grunting *"Et tu Brute?"*[3]

More people kept coming, including most of the women who had remained at the *muvunga* tree. I even spotted Mukoma's wife, Maiguru MaMoyo, in the crowd. I had thought she was too disappointed in Mukoma to think of becoming one of the spectators, but there she was, finally, swaying in response to the flights of fists. She clapped her hands, and raised her small fist in the air each time Mukoma punched. A few of the women started ululating, while some men whistled. The fighters began throwing merciless punches. Still, Mukoma and Jakove had the upper hand, releasing blows faster than the brothers. I tried to move

---

3   *Et tu Brute?* - And you too Brutus?

closer, but someone pushed me, and a struggle ensued that ejected me out of the crowd altogether. I stood clear of the crowd and concentrated on an arriving group, which consisted mainly of teachers and more students. I even saw Enias, who had removed his Mark Anthony costume, dragging his feet as if he had been forced to come to the fight, and behind him the soothsayer limped. I hid behind someone so these two wouldn't see me.

I didn't want to watch the fight anymore, so I started walking away. I had barely left the crowd when I saw my English teacher, Miss Mukaro, walking slowly towards the scene. She saw me too, slowed down, then stopped. Her face looked concerned but indifferent, as if the fight didn't interest her. I was ready to hear her opinion about the fight, but, I greeted her nervously, and she nodded to show her understanding that the fight was not my fault.

We stood quietly under a mulberry tree not very far from the crowd, her arms crossed, as if she was hugging herself. I was waiting for her to say something, but I didn't want her to express her sympathy for me. That would ruin my day. It was one thing to know my teacher cared, and another to hear her words of sympathy.

"Does he do this all the time?" she said, her voice muffled by the crowd's din. Then her voice dropped. "I'm sorry if I'm asking too many questions."

I actually found her question refreshing, but I just shook my head to indicate that his fights were not frequent, to show that I was just as surprised as she was. I didn't want to say something that would make her change her mind on meeting with Mukoma. She gazed into my eyes, as if she was checking for traces of something I wasn't saying. This was her signature technique in the classroom, to get us to give the best of our answers. I felt the intensity of her stare and I couldn't bear it. I looked away.

"Don't worry, Fati," she said. "You didn't plan for this to happen." I felt a knot in my throat and my eyes began to burn, but crying was out of the question. We — Mukoma and I — were not the crying type. You just dealt with situations like a man. Besides, that wouldn't look good in front of a lady. I looked at the ground and for a moment forgot that I was a Form Three student, but felt more like a sulking Grade Seven boy waiting for an adult to make important decisions for him, someone telling me not to worry, because there was always a better day in life. In moments like this, I always reminded myself that I was an orphan and was fortunate to have Mukoma, who had raised me as if I was his own son. Miss Mukaro knew that I had no parents and respected the fact that Mukoma had tried his best to educate me.

I wasn't worrying about anything. I don't know why she thought I was worrying. I straightened and looked at the roaring crowd too. I was too aware of my teacher's presence that although I could see the excited crowd, I wasn't reading much into what they were doing. For the first time, standing with Miss Mukaro felt strange, as if I had just met her.

Her silence was beginning to make me uncomfortable. She didn't have to take it out on me or think anything less of me. I didn't want to change her mind on the offer she had made to me. If I passed my O-Level next year, she would sponsor part of my A-Level studies. It had only been two weeks since we had the discussion. At the end of rehearsals for the play, she had walked with me and my friends on our way home. She was going to Vhazhure shopping centre, which was on our side of the village.

"So what line of work are you thinking of doing when you finish school?" she had asked me.

I opened my mouth and closed it without saying anything. I didn't know what work people did after O-Level. I knew what people without O-Level did — security guard, store clerk, mine worker, farm worker, bus conductor, train ticket checker. I had never quite connected my school qualifications with work. I just enjoyed going to school and getting good grades, making my brother proud.

"Do you, for instance, see yourself in the sciences, becoming an apprentice or something related?" Miss Mukaro asked.

I hadn't thought about that either, but I had an idea. Mukoma had told me that he had once wanted to become a highly paid electrician or mechanical engineer had his education not been cut short by the death of our father. I got the sense then that he was hinting that since he had not been able to do it, I should do it for our family. But even as he spoke, I had not found much interest in the fields he was talking about, so I hadn't paid much attention. Besides, I wasn't going to tell Miss Mukaro about dreams of becoming a scientist since she was my English teacher and I was one of her best students. Instead, I said, "I'll definitely find something in the English area or in writing, professional acting maybe, if there is such a thing." I was going to add that I might consider becoming a teacher like her, but she shook her head and started laughing her soft kind of laughter.

"I wish it was that easy for those of us who love English," she said, "to easily become just writers and actors." She paused. "I wouldn't discourage your dreams for writing and acting, but in order to have better chances in these areas, you need to go to A-Level and proceed to university. You're so talented and diligent, and I would hate to see your education stopping here in the village. Do you want to go to A-Level?"

"I do, but I don't think my brother can afford the fees." I then regretted having told her about what my brother wasn't prepared to do, so I added, "He has done a lot for me so far, and I'm grateful for it."

She nodded and walked on silently. I walked by her side feeling hesitant, hoping no one would see us together since we were getting close to my turn-off.

"Maybe, I can help," she said, "if you really want to go to A-Level."

"I want to go to A-Level," I said.

My sudden response seemed to surprise her, but then she smiled widely and said, "I'm serious. I understand your situation. We were just talking about you last week with Andrews. You should hear what she thinks of you, bragging about you and calling you Oxford material."

I wondered if my Science teacher expected me to become a scientist after O-Level. And I wondered what Oxford material was, but I didn't ask Miss Mukaro to explain. I didn't want to interrupt her. "And look, even Andrews who is an expatriate can see the talent in you, but we don't want to make the mistake of allowing foreigners to discover our own talent if we are intelligent enough to discover it ourselves." She paused and looked at me directly in the eye, as if expecting me to show a sign that I agreed with her on the issue of foreigners discovering our talent. I smiled, and she smiled back and said, "I'm serious, Fati. I will make sure that you are discovered and nurtured. I hate it when smart students miss on opportunities because of circumstances they can't control."

I nodded.

"Even how you write poems and other things says a lot about your potential," she said, focusing her attention to a noisy flock of birds that was passing above us.

I wasn't only writing poems and other things; I had a whole novel, two plays and nine short stories. She knew this; she had read my novel.

"I guarantee that if you were at a city school, you would already have been noticed by a wider audience," she said. "All your novels would be at College Press…you know, Longman, but I bet you don't even know what those are."

"Are they publishing houses?"

"Exactly what I was saying: you know way too much for anyone to watch you amounting to nothing in this arid village."

She was saying things that touched me. I didn't quite like how she seemed to imply that my village was just an arid place with nothing to offer, but I liked that she knew something about my writing. Then I pictured myself in Harare or Bulawayo, at a school where everyone would talk about me, and my name in newspapers. But then the sight of Chisiya Hill, with goats limping as they always did at sunset, brought me to the reality of Mhototi and the clumps of trees forming the pattern of Runde River valley, and then the bald, bluish Gweshumba Mountains in the distance. Ah, even the gravel that we walked on seemed to murmur its disapproval of my wayward thoughts. I coughed nervously, getting ready to tell her that I was going to take my exit soon.

But when the turn-off came, we stood by the roadside for over thirty minutes, talking about higher education and its benefits. On that day, it was decided that if the help was needed, she would pay for a greater part of my A-Level. And if Mukoma could not come with the rest, only then would she consider approaching other teachers, such as the British expatriate, to chip in, but she would be the main source of help. I couldn't believe that she had made this offer to me who was not her relative, but it made me feel happier than I had ever felt before, made me think I could do something important with my education beyond Mhototi.

And now, to have this fight happen here on school grounds on a day Miss Mukaro was planning to talk with Mukoma!

I didn't want to answer Miss Mukaro's question. Of course, Mukoma fought all the time, but I didn't want to tell his business to my teachers. If she really wanted to know, if her question was serious, she would have to make up her mind and reach her own conclusion. If this meant that she was interested in meeting Mukoma today as she had planned, she alone could make that choice. And, as for her sponsorship of my A-Level, if that ended up not happening because of this fight... what could I do? What could anyone do?

I leaned against the tree and looked at the sky.

"Are you OK?" she asked, coming closer to me."

"I'm fine," I said. "It's just that..." I couldn't say it. I forgot what I wanted to say, so I just looked at my feet, at the tire sandals I had worn to pretend I was wearing Roman sandals. The British Council had been out of Roman sandals to use in our play, so Miss Andrews and Miss Mukaro had said I could wear any shoes I had, and these tire sandals were my pair of shoes at the time. Mukoma had said he would look into buying me a pair of real shoes once his job situation got better. His situation, whatever it was, when it got better, he would buy the real shoes.

"You don't have to talk about it," Miss Mukaro said, returning her stare to the restless crowd.

We stood in silence for a while. I suppressed any thoughts about the fight and focused on how my play about this fight would begin, if I were to write one in the future what disguise I would use for the Mukoma character. I had just ticked myself into thinking about the fight which I was trying to avoid. I then tried to imagine what Miss Mukaro's childhood had been like, who her first boyfriend had been..., but I coudn't think such thoughts about my teacher. No one knew if Miss Mukaro had a man in her life...

Our silence and stillness became too oppressive. She looked as if she was now upset with me. Shutting off the noise from the crowd, I cast my stare down to my sandals again. My toes were tapping on the rubber base, feeling its roughness. They moved on their own accord, without my control, as if they were up to something I didn't know. She probably wasn't thinking of helping me anymore. And Mukoma had already told me twice that he may not be able to pay even for my O-Level examinations. Dreaming about A-Level was pointless if no one was going to pay for my examinations next year. Then if Miss Mukaro wasn't going to introduce herself to Mukoma today, she may not feel like she had the authorisation to help me, and without anyone's help I was just going to grow old and die useless in the village, leaving no legacy, no name, no contribution, just a piece of cow's dung, useless, useless, useless... Maybe, yes, I could work for someone, in their field, if Mukoma allowed me, to raise my examination fees. But he wouldn't allow me to do such a thing, having always said even though we were poor, we were not beggars and no one in Mhototi was allowed to dare try to help me. I was afraid that even though he and Miss Mukaro would meet today, he might say no to her offer but, at least, a meeting was better than nothing, and now…the shouts of the crazy crowd —*you blocks, you stones…worse than senseless things* — shouting in unbidden flourish!

"So why did you leave the fight?" Miss Mukaro asked. "It's your brother… nothing wrong with watching."

"No, I would rather be here than there," I said, shaking my head and trying to control my quavering voice.

She smiled… no, that wasn't a smile, but just a parting of the lips and a brief flash of the teeth, yet even with this ambiguous emotion, she still looked wise. So then, yes, she was smiling. I smiled back, a dry, painful smile.

"Everyone looks so entertained," she said. "It's like a tournament for them." She nodded. "Happy people, all on account of your brother."

"And the Mhere boys," I said. She turned sharply to look at me, looking confused.

"That's what everyone calls them, since a long time ago."

"I see," she said. "So they're like a gang then?"

I didn't know what to say.

"Like a group of thugs, so to speak," she explained.

"No, just brothers," I said. "Real close brothers."

She broke into laughter, thin peals that she was struggling to control. "There goes the literature man again," she said between gusts of her laughter. "Well, we've our brother in there too. Don't we have to support him?"

Our brother? Something tugged at my heart, as if, suddenly, I had just discovered the sister I never had. Maybe she was our sister. Maybe she and Mukoma knew what I didn't know, and they were planning to surprise me today. Maybe Maiguru knew too, about Miss Mukaro being the sister I never knew about. But this very thought was silly, so I swatted it by saying, "I hate fights on school grounds."

The crowd burst open, and one Mhere boy shot out and ran by where we stood, holding his head. He slowed down, looked at us as if he was about to explain something but suddenly picked speed and ran towards the Gwavachemai Mountains. Two men ran after him, shouting.

"Hey, come back here! The fight is not over." But they gave up, stood and looked at us, shook their heads, then ran back to the crowd.

"That was one of the four brothers," I said. "Maybe he's going to get some weapons."

"Weapons?" she asked.

"A knobkerrie, an axe, or spear," I said. "They usually bring such weapons, although I've never seen them using them."

"Strange," she said, shaking her head as if the whole of Mhototi disappointed her.

She's not going to meet with Mukoma, nor is she going to help me, I thought.

"That man is in bad shape," she said.

"Mukoma worked on him real good," I said, then quickly covered my mouth.

She laughed. "You're right, he looks quite worked on." After a moment she said, "So brother is a good fighter then?" Before I answered she added, "I guess that's obvious, now the question is: how good of a fighter are you?"

"I'm Caesar," I said, getting in character again.

We laughed. She didn't ask more questions about Mukoma after that. We stood there for a moment without saying anything. With one Mhere boy gone, the match was now three to two. The screams of the crowd increased, the din was maddening.

"We better go watch this performance too," she said, walking. "I hate fights!"

"So do I," I said, following her. I stayed behind her, not wanting people to see me walking side by side with her. Although she kept turning around as if she wanted to check if I was following, she didn't seem to mind that I trailed behind her.

There was no good spot to see the fight from, no matter how hard we tried to find one. I didn't want to be separated from the teacher, so I just followed what she was doing, let her try to open room for us, maybe people would recognise her and open some room for us, but no one did, no one paid us any attention.

The crowd stirred in response to the sudden sound of whistles coming from the east of the school. Muturu, Makokova and Tukano, the men who volunteered as security guards for our school, tore towards the crowd. Behind them were the headmaster, his deputy and the sports- master. The crowd started to disperse. Even Miss Mukaro and I joined those escaping the scene. I knew the fight was not going to stop. For one, the security guards knew and respected Mukoma as a fighter. What I didn't know was how Mukoma and Jakove would react upon seeing them, but this was not for me to worry about. Miss Mukaro and I sank deeper into the crowd, speeding back to the *muvunga* tree. Some people had remained at the fight, but the majority, mostly women and the elderly, had left.

Back at the tree, Baba Mugwevi, the chairman of the Parents Teachers Association, was addressing the crowd, talking even as more people arrived and as some kept turning their heads in the direction of the fight. I kept turning in that direction too, now worried about what was happening to Mukoma and Jakove. Were they going to be arrested? I didn't want other students to know that my brother had gotten in trouble. I caught only fragments of Baba Mugwevi's words: "… future of your children…your future…" I wanted to run back to the scene of the fight to alert Mukoma of the arrival of the security guards, but I didn't know what Miss Mukaro would think. I didn't want to leave her sitting there alone. Well, I could, but I didn't want her to think that I was a bad student. I sat still, and listened to the speaker.

"The children here were showing us something important," Baba Mugwevi said. "Then some grown men who seem to have forgotten what grown-up means, acted like fools. Don't do that to your children; don't do that to yourselves, people!"

The crowd applauded. But the applause stopped when we saw the security guards arriving. They walked with an air of confidence and victory; it became clear that they had stopped the fight. I sighed with relief because it seemed Mukoma and Jakove were not in serious trouble; the guards were smiling. But shouldn't they be dragging the Mhere boys? Was the fight still going on? Usually, fighters or troublemakers were taken to the little security office at the school, to be questioned further; then if there was no resolution, the Zvishavane police would be called. Although Zvishavane was forty kilometres away, it was the nearest town with a police station that served the villages of Mazvihwa. The police usually took hours to arrive, but once they did, an arrest was guaranteed. No one here ever wanted to see those police. I didn't want Mukoma to get into trouble.

As I listened to Baba Mugwevi, I kept looking for Mukoma and Jakove. "Mhototi should be proud to have such talented children as these, who bring us stories set in distant places, but today we cannot be proud because of grown men who act like children. We have children with big dreams, children working hard in school so that they can take care of us one day." More applause. "Mhototi, this is your children's future... it is only you who will suffer if you don't allow them to realise their dreams. This...", but he was interrupted by more applause.

Miss Mukaro nodded rapidly, turned to me and said, "It's good that the play will go on."

"Great news," I said, but I didn't feel like performing anymore, even though I would be a corpse in the remaining scenes of the play.

****

98

Suddenly, all heads turned as VaMukamuri, the headmaster, appeared and walked to the stage slowly, counting his paces. He stopped only to allow Baba Mugwevi to descend from the platform. They exchanged glances and nodded at each other. Silence descended and anticipation filled the air.

The headmaster climbed the platform and cleared his throat. "Parents, guardians and students," he said, "I'm not here to dwell on what the fighters did or did not do, but I would like the students to be given a chance to finish their performance; that's why we are here, and it shall be as we had planned."

There was general applause, which was suddenly interrupted by the arrival of Mukoma and Jakove. They walked to the headmaster, and Jakove whispered something to him. The headmaster's face lit with a smile and he lifted his voice: "We are going to hear a word or two from our heroes here. But before we do, let's respect the students and allow them to finish their play. We have a long programme, and little time to complete it in." He then turned to Mukoma and Jakove and said, "Thank you gentlemen for dealing with this problem." Then he left the platform and joined them, and together, they walked to the back of the crowd. Miss Mukaro stood up, and as she walked up to the front, I could feel confusion finally gripping me like a disease. Scanning the crowd, I located the other actors, scattered in different spots, confusion or fear registered on their faces.

Snakes Will Follow You

I was lying on a reed mat in the shade of a *tsapi*[1] hut, reading *Julius Caesar*. As soon as Brutus stabbed Caesar, I looked up to avoid picturing the pain. That's when I saw a baby snake wriggling towards me. I jumped and screamed, but muffled the scream as soon as I remembered I was a man. Not any man, but one trained by my big brother, Mukoma, to be a man in all situations. I hoped that Maiguru, his wife, who was cooking in the kitchen hut, had not heard me, so I stiffened and watched the snake as it slithered towards me. I wanted to give it time to finish its mission; then I would trap it between the pages of *Shakespeare*.

When it reached the edge of the mat, it coiled into a neat wheel. My heart was beating faster, but I moved closer to examine it. It was shiny black with white lines and tiny green eyes that looked at me with some recognition. Those eyes were adorable, as if the snake had decided to become my pet, or that it was wooing me to be part of its world. It was just a baby though, but one could never trust a snake. I began to suspect that it was not alone, so I tiptoed backwards to remove myself from the possible danger that the snake could be a sign of a warning or an omen. The date wasn't March 15, but who was to say that there were no *ides* of April?

It must have noticed that I was trying to escape because it uncoiled and slid towards me again. I moved faster, but bumped against the wall behind me. It advanced and seemed as though it was transforming and growing bigger. I pinched my eyes shut and when I reopened them, the small snake was advancing slowly, as if it had all day to follow me. I hurled the book at it — oh, my *Julias Caesar* — which covered all but its tail. The tail wriggled for a few seconds before it lay limp. It must be dead, I thought as I felt saliva filling my mouth. I spat and tiptoed

---

1   *tsapi* - a store-chamber of grain at a homestead in a rural setting

closer. I paused to check for a movement, of the book or the tail, but there was none. Feeling safe, I pushed the book aside with my big toe and jumped back, but remembered to remain courageous. I lowered myself to a crouch and examined the snake. Its head was now squashed and the rest of its body lay stuck to the ground. I sighed in victory.

I called Maiguru and she came out running. She was covered in sweat, from the cooking, and had the look she always gave me when she thought I was being silly, that sideways, eyes-down look of hers.

"What happened?" she said. "I thought I heard you scream but remembered that sometimes you read out loud."

She was going to step on the snake.

"Watch out!" I said.

She stopped, looked on the ground and then stumbled backwards. After she regained her balance, she said, "The prophet told you already."

"Yes, but this..."

She raised her hand to silence me. "He was clear: until you leave the village, this is what will happen."

"Even baby ones too?" I said, following her gaze, which seemed to track the trail of the snake.

She turned back to me and dropped her shoulders in disappointment. "Did it try to follow you? Did you try to run?"

"I don't run from baby snakes," I said, pumping up my shoulders. "I don't run from snakes, full stop."

She clicked her tongue in deprecation. "This is not a test of your manhood, Babamunini. If a prophet says a thing, you have to listen to that prophet." Then she clasped her hands together and started chewing her lips like she was ready to solve a puzzle.

The prophet! Of course, had told me about snakes acting funny, but how was I supposed to know that they would try to disturb my studies like this? I was just a student who didn't bother anybody. What did they — the witches, the snakes, even the prophets or whatever want from me who had nothing to offer except a bunch of books? Besides, I didn't know what the prophet had called the "events" would start this soon. He had said I would have some headaches first; then the snakes would come. But if Maiguru was right, it seemed the snakes had beaten the headaches.

Maiguru bent to take a closer look at the snake. She started nodding the way she did when she thought only she understood what was going on. "Yes, this is the kind that would follow you around. It is the innocent kind that witches will send."

"*Ya*?[2] And you know this, how?" I asked.

"My ears, unlike those of someone I know, were open when the prophet talked," she said. "And I think this is just a warning. This is them being nice."

"Them?"

"You know, witches, who else?" Her face darkened, like something was biting her insides. "Do you even care about all this? About your safety?" She was breathing heavily. "If they succeed, even these little books you are reading will all go to waste because graves don't write examinations, or do they?"

I pretended I had not heard that question and went back to her idea of a warning. "So it's saying watch out for what may happen in April?" I said, stopping short of mentioning Julius Caesar and his *ides* because, with Maiguru, it would just be a waste of time. She just didn't have a clue about literature, and sometimes I thought she was better off not knowing, just as she always told me that there were things I was safe not knowing.

"It could be any month," she said, straightening and fixing her skirt which had started crawling up her body. Maybe it was already hitched that high when she bolted out of the hut. She always fixed her skirt that way when she was cooking. She frowned and I looked away. "It could be any day," she said. "Just be careful."

---

2   *Ya?* - Is that so?

I nodded and picked up my book. I looked for stains and although I did not see any, I wiped it on my shirt, but immediately stopped when Maiguru raised her hand in protest.

"No, you don't do that!" she said.

"Do what?" I said, looking to see if my free hand was doing anything it shouldn't be doing.

"I don't think you should be the first one to touch that book." She dashed forward, closer, her hand extended. "Give it to me, let me touch it first. If they choose to follow me, that's better. You are in school, I am not."

"But I have already touched it," I said.

"Just pretend you didn't touch it and let me be the one to touch it first," she said.

There was no way I would let her take my book. I needed to continue reading. She didn't seem to realise that I was not afraid of baby snakes, I was neither afraid of the snakes nor the witches! I had an examination on *Julius Caesar* on the next day and this was not the time to worry about witches.

When she saw that I would not relent, she dropped her hands. She then shook her head the way Mukoma did if he thought I had not completed a task properly, a shake of the head that always led to my sound beating. I resented Maiguru for shaking her head like that. She did not have the authority to act like Mukoma to me, and even if she had, I was too old to be controlled.

I leaned against the hut and started flipping through the pages, although my eyes kept looking at her. I was curious to see what she was going to do with the snake. I wasn't going to touch it. She could touch the snake if she had to be the first one to touch something.

"You are lucky you saw it before it got into you," she said.

I raised my head and looked at her directly. She was wiping sweat from her upper lip.

"What are you talking about now?" I asked her, but she looked away. If we could talk of anything getting inside anyone, shouldn't we be talking about her? The thought itself made me shudder: I couldn't afford to have her suspect that I had such dirty thoughts about her. I normally didn't think of her in these terms. She was like a mother to me. And, of course, Mukoma would kill me if he ever suspected that I thought such nonsense.

As if she had read my thoughts, Maiguru said, "Silly you. Always thinking about dirty things. You forget that, that's not good behaviour for a junior deacon?"

That was another thing: my being a junior deacon was all new to me, even the church-going thing itself. And now the talk of witches making snakes follow me. Sometimes I forgot about being a deacon altogether, thinking about my upcoming examinations. Then the prophet, shouldn't he have chosen a better time to tell me about my enemies? How did Maiguru even know that I was thinking about dirty things? Now, was she turning into a prophet too?

She started pacing about like a prophet, no... like a *n'anga,* circling around the snake in a ritual I did not want to understand at this time. So I opened my book and found Caesar falling, but I was brought back to the snake when she said, "A snake this small can enter you and live in your stomach to eat your food. With the way you eat nowadays, I think you already have something in you." She pointed at my stomach with her small finger, but her eyes were still on the dead snake.

These original theories of hers, which were nowhere near scientific, always left me speechless.

"I eat a lot because I didn't eat a lot when I was ill; that's all," I said.

"You don't know that," she said, her voice signalling that she knew she was right and nothing I said would change her position. "Sometimes you have to let yourself know only what those who see what you can't see tell you..."

"I know," I said, cutting her off. "It's just that I have to catch up on the work that others did all the months I was away."

"You will take care of that in Harare," she said, lowering her voice on the word Harare, like she didn't want me to go anymore, which was possible. But because she was right that I could do a better job of catching up on my studies in Harare, I smiled and closed the book. As soon as Mukoma confirmed that I could come, which I knew he would eventually, I would be gone from Mazvihwa for a long, long time. I was getting tired of prophecies about witches and snakes. I was tired of getting sick all the time and missing school.

I doubted that I had a snake inside me, but Maiguru was right about what the prophet from Nhenga, our church's headquarters, had said. He told me that since I had been blessed to recover from my long illness, which had made me miss school for all of February and March, and since I was scheduled to write my examinations in November, I had to leave the village for Harare, where my brother worked. Either that, or, as the prophet had offered, move to Nhenga temporarily, and only return when it was time to write the examinations. The Harare option, which depended on Mukoma finding sense in what the prophet had said, was my best option.

He also explained the cause of other symptoms of my illness; the headache, he said, was the work of demons, and that could easily be taken care of by exposure to the steam of boiling holy water, which I had done and felt better; the stomach-ache resulted from eating poisoned food, but the prayers at the evangelist's in Mariwowo had helped heal that, and then there were the muscle spasms on the chest. He said a witch had inserted snake flesh in my chest while I slept. This, he said, would attract more snakes, which would start to follow me, which could pose great danger since there was no telling what harm the snakes would cause and how soon, so I needed to watch where I walked, where I sat, where I shat even, and where I slept. But he had said nothing about snakes entering my stomach. Well, maybe he had, but I was still recovering from a long illness then, and half the time I did not hear what he was saying since I was dozing. Good thing Maiguru had been there to listen in as well. But the details, even for the junior deacon side of me, were dubious. And, as a human driven by mere flesh, what was to stop me from doubting, like Thomas? Or, to be a little arrogant like Caesar, the invincible, whose name even death feared? I puffed out my chest and started walking.

Maiguru jumped and screamed.

"What?" I said, dashing closer to the snake.

"Did you see it? It moved!" she said, holding her mouth, her eyes opening wider.

"I don't think it moved," I said, drawing even closer, like a man.

"Burn it!" she said, pointing at it with both hands. "Burn this work of Satan!"

"Didn't you say you wanted to cook it?" I said, laughing.

"You have jokes," she said, rolling her eyes. I hated it when she did that because it made me think that she thought she was my age and was trying to seduce me.

"No, seriously I thought it was your baby," I said.

She frowned and looked away again. A thought struck me and I knew I had gone too far. I suddenly began to feel bad.

"I didn't mean to say that, Maiguru," I said.

She turned to look at me with a tilted, pensive face. That worsened how I felt. I shouldn't have made the baby joke, especially in the context of the snake and prophecy.

Her ten-year marriage to Mukoma had not yielded a baby, which is why she had joined the church shortly after I did. The prophets told her that with Wedenga[3] anything was possible, and they recommended, commanded even, that she go to Nhenga, four or five times in a row, each time spending a week or two, in order to become pregnant. She

---

3   Wedenga - Of the heavens. Another Shona name for God.

106

could only be treated in Nhenga, but, like me, she had to check with Mukoma if that was something she could do.

Maybe Mukoma would ask me to accompany her to Nhenga instead of going to live with him in Harare. The worst that could happen was that he would beat both of us for following the orders of a prophet, and he would not allow me to go either to Harare or Nhenga. He would probably beat Maiguru and send her back to her family, temporarily, to send a strong message. Maiguru's worst fear was that he would be infuriated and take a second wife. Or a third one since Maiguru already suspected he had another wife in the city. But Maiguru had already told me she would go to Nhenga for treatment, even if she had to do so secretly. As for what would end up happening, to go or not to go, we just had to wait for Mukoma to arrive in two weeks. In the meantime, I had to set things right with Maiguru.

"I am sorry," I said.

"You are what?" she asked and started walking away.

"I didn't mean what I said," I said, following her, not caring about the snake anymore.

She stopped, looked on the ground, and pondered; in fact, she started grinding her teeth, a thing that always sounded painful. She must really have been hurt by what I said.

"You didn't say anything," she said, licking her lower lip; then a smile lit her face. "But burn the snake, Babamunini."

"I will do so right away," I said, offering her my book, which she waved away. "I am going to light up a fire."

"No, just douse it in paraffin and light a match. Delaying will cause its mother to smell its death and come after you."

"You are making sense, Maiguru," I said.

She nodded and left me standing there as she went back into the kitchen hut. As she entered the kitchen she shouted, without turning, "Hurry up too or the food will get cold."

"Food!" I shouted and took off like a little boy towards the firewood pile.

The thing did not take time to burn. I buried the ashes in the sweet potato plot and drew a cross on the mound of red soil I had smoothened. I took my book and entered the kitchen hut where a plate of *sadza* and catfish waited for me. Maiguru laughed at me when I closed and bolted the door. Although I could sense forgiveness in that laughter, the worst was yet to come.

Little Wife

Vonai arrived on a Sunday. She told us she just wanted to see her aunt, Maiguru MaMoyo, show her that she had matured and could explore Harare on her own. That's how she had found our house in Glen View 2.

"Like that?" said Maiguru. "Just started looking and here you are?"

"You can say I did that, *tete*,"[1] said Vonai, smiling. "All I needed were the smallest details."

She looked at me sideways, beaming, suggesting the *varamu*[2] seductiveness, something I wasn't quite used to; besides, my religion would not permit me to touch the breasts of a woman I wasn't married to. So, in short, I wasn't into that *varamu* stuff.

"You needed the smallest detail… like, say, an address?" I said, to confuse her since she wasn't that educated. Maiguru coughed out a brief laugh.

"Something like that," Vonai said, rolling her eyes at me. "Someone gave me the address a long time ago. And I found myself using it today."

She sat on a couch across from me, and I struggled to keep my eyes away from her already exposed thigh. She noticed and fixed her skirt. I felt bad for being caught looking. I wasn't one of those up-skirt perverts.

Maiguru shook her head. She didn't like the idea of people from the village showing up unannounced. But Vonai was her niece.

"Tell me, how did you make it all the way here?" she asked. "The last time I talked to your father he said no one knew where you were."

"He didn't know?" Vonai said. "That's strange." She grimaced and leaned forward.

"Are you saying he knew?" said Maiguru. "He was angry and didn't want to talk to me."

Vonai tossed her head back and laughed. Maiguru frowned and said, "You think this is funny?"

---

1   *tete* - aunt
2   *varamu* - the wife's nieces or younger sisters. Culturally, *varamu* are regarded as the husband's junior 'wives'. The husband's brothers (younger and older) also regard varamu as their junior wives.

Vonai stopped laughing and her eyes opened wider then narrowed, as if they were being moved by waves of guilt.

As if she wanted to make sure that Vonai's laughter had truly stopped, Maiguru remained silent for a while, and then said, "You don't tell people where you are and the next minute they start expecting someone will show up with bride price."

"He thought I was married?" Vonai said, looking at her fingers, counting them. Her whole demeanor softened, but there was a troubled look on her face. She looked at Maiguru and said, "He was not too wrong then." She raised her face and laughed briefly. Her mouth hung open like that exposing some fine teeth.

Maiguru and I sat up simultaneously. I could tell Maiguru was getting upset. I was getting excited.

"Tell me where you were, right now, Vonai," Maiguru said. She leaned forward, her lips trembling.

"I was out and about, doing this and that." Vonai shifted on the sofa, as if something had pinched her. I looked away. "Now I'm sure you are happy, Auntie, that I found you."

Maiguru cleared her throat and assumed an authoritative tone. "I knew that you were up to no good when your father said he didn't know where you were. Now you just show up at my door unanounced. What do you want me to do with you?"

Vonai let a smile linger on her face. For the first time, I noticed her beauty, but I didn't really care about it, so I looked past her to the window, where the curtains flapped in the late afternoon breeze.

"Auntie, things have not been easy, but, you know, we try." There was pride in her voice now. I noticed too that she had switched to sporadic English, now calling Maiguru "auntie" instead of 'tete'. And she sounded... good... sexy, saying things in English. It was hard though to imagine what type of "trying" a person of her low, or rather modest education and age could talk about.

"I know you try, and now you are trying not to answer all my questions," Maiguru said. "Speak in Shona[4] too. I'm not your friend." She then looked at me and I started nodding for I knew she was right; she understood how these teenagers behaved.

"Questions are answered always, *tete*," Vonai said.

"So start making sense, or I will ask you to leave right away! I don't want trouble in my house." Maiguru paused to look around the room, which was all there was to what we called our house. "You know how your father is."

"You want to hear the truth?" Vonai said, her eyes directed to me.

"Would you dare lie to me?" Maiguru said. "And why are you looking at Babamunini and not me?"

Vonai turned and looked at Maiguru directly. "I'm just trying to respect you, Auntie," she said. "And just so you know, Babamunini is the one looking at me. He thinks I haven't noticed." She started laughing, which turned the climate in the room playful again. Even Maiguru laughed.

Vonai told us that when everyone back in the village was wondering what had happened to her, she had been in Kariba.

"Kariba? That's too far from home," Maiguru said. "Who just gets up and goes to Kariba?"

"A man was going to marry me, I'm not going to lie to you, Tete," Vonai said, stretching her neck and shaking her short brown braids, and giving me a special stare, added, "Or, shall we say: I was going to marry a man?" I laughed, but killed the laughter by clearing my throat.

Vonai turned her eyes to Maiguru, ignoring my laughter. She had a nice side profile too, good bone structure.

"Then what happened to you and the man?" Maiguru asked, pouting.

"I woke up one day and decided to leave. I had resold some fish I bought from a white man at the lake, and I made enough money for transport, and said, 'Where is my auntie again?' My heart told me, 'Go to Harare.' So, here I am." She grinned with satisfaction.

---

4   Shona - one of the main indigenous languages spoken in Zimbabwe by the Shona tribe

"That's not a story," I said, clapping. "Technically."

"What's a story to you, Mr Book?" she said, rolling her eyes.

"You have to tell me more than that, Voni," Maiguru said. "So you were in Kariba, you wanted to marry a man. Where had you met this man?"

"He met me," she said. She sat up straight and pulled down her blouse that had kept crawling up to expose her light-toned stomach, and as she covered the stomach fully, her chest, cleavage, that is, got exposed some more. I sank deeper into the sofa and pretended not to stare.

Maiguru said, "He found you? But you're not telling me where."

"I really don't want to waste your time with the details, Auntie. But one day I was in Zvishavane behind the counter of a little grocery store near Mandava and the next thing I was in a rich man's Toyota going to Kariba." She paused as if to wonder at the thought of the car headed for Kariba. "He was a nice man, was going to pay a lot of money for my *roora*,[5] then throw the best wedding on earth." She looked on the floor as if that's where the wedding could have been thrown. Then she started shaking her head slowly. There was something sad in the way her head swayed, thrusting the short braids. But my eyes remembered what was worth looking at. When she stopped shaking her head, she glanced at me, darkened her face and pulled her blouse, leaving the stomach exposed again. "This life, Auntie, I tell you, it's something else," she said.

"Tell me about it," said Maiguru, examining the exposed stomach. She probably was thinking what I was thinking, but it was too flat for that.

"So this man, he took you to Kariba in his car. And then what?" Maiguru said.

"Things didn't work out as planned, so then everything happened as I already said, and the best decision I ever made was to think of you,

---

5   *roora* - bride price

Tete." She widened her eyes as if she had just discovered her aunt, the way David Livingstone discovered Victoria Falls. "And here I am, with you, with Babamunini here, and soon, Babamukuru will be home, right?"

"You're here, I can see that, but you know I have no room for you," Maiguru said. "Why didn't you write in advance to tell us you were coming?" She looked at me as if to show that I was part of "us." "A warning would have prepared us better."

I laughed at Maiguru's use of the word warning, as if Vonai was a plague or a hurricane.

"I didn't write because…I just didn't," Vonai said. "But the plans got better on the bus from Kariba to here!"

"You met another man," Maiguru said. "Meeting them must be your hobby."

"No-o, just a family returning from a weekend trip," she said. "There are people who can still afford to take trips to fun places, Auntie."

"You met a family on a bus…okay?" Maiguru kept her mouth open.

"We started talking and one topic led to another and then they employed me on the spot to be a maid." She paused. "They insisted on calling me a domestic relative though."

"Ah!" I said. I was beginning to like her sense of humour.

"They promised me good money, so I took the offer and told myself, 'Now I don't have to burden my aunt, but I can visit her often.' So here I am."

Indeed, she was here, her whole sixteen-year-old self. She looked more attractive, but I didn't care much about that. I cared more about my books, about scholarships, universities and all that. And about Jesus, of course, especially about Jesus. I looked away from her.

"So where does this family of yours live?" Maiguru said.

"Oh, we live in Glen View," she said, pointing in what she supposed was the direction of Glen View, but she had pointed in the direction of Mbudzi cemetery. Maiguru and I didn't say anything, so she continued,

"She is a nice woman. She has two children who attend school in town. The husband lives alone somewhere but sometimes comes to visit for a night or two."

"Some messed up family right there," I said.

"They are not a family anymore."

"You are not making sense, Vonai," Maiguru said.

"The man is no longer her husband, but again they are not divorced. It's weird how she explained it. All I care about is my job. She pays me well."

There was silence in the room. I pictured a dysfunctional family where the husband sneaked in at midnight and left before everyone woke up, and I wondered how the woman felt about all this; and then Vonai, in that house, taking care of two spoilt children. Brats who probably believed they were in America or some such place they saw on TV. Vonai working, slaving away her sixteen years, perhaps attracting that weird man, and thinking she was grown up, when what she should focus on was her education and, of course, church. I was in A-Level and had not even started to worry about women and work. But she was actually employed, she was making money…and I was not… Perhaps I could borrow some money from her one day. The thought made me smile, but I restrained myself.

Maiguru appeared to be thinking about something serious too, while Vonai looked at her hands, then at me, a satisfied expression on her face. Yes, I will borrow some money from her one day.

Finally, Maiguru coughed in her cupped hand, and said, "Just make sure that man doesn't touch you."

"He wouldn't even dare," Vonai said. She blinked rapidly, and while scratching her chin, said, "Would he?"

"You tell me," Maiguru said. "Wouldn't he?"

"What do you think, Babamunini?" Vonai asked. "Would the man dare touch me?" Then she burst out laughing, looking at the ceiling.

114

Maiguru and I looked at each other. I shook my head and said, "I don't know." Just then I became aware, again, of her cleavage. I looked away and heard Maiguru say, "Behave, Vonai. And be careful with these men."

There was a moment of silence, which was suddenly broken by Maiguru's hum. Vonai looked at me and said, "So Babamunini, how have you been?"

"You know, just trying my best to contribute to life in a positive way," I said, pointing at a pile of books: Shakespeare, Faulkner, Sparks and some journal exercise books.

"You still write things?" she asked, and I could detect sarcasm in her voice.

"Things? You must mean novels," I said, thickening my voice.

"Whatever." She looked at her right thumbnail suddenly, as if something had just happened to it, then while averting her eyes to the roof, said, "You think I care whether it's novels or things? There is more to life than books."

"Don't be rude to this man now," said Maiguru. "He is as good as your husband! Have manners, Vonai!" Maiguru was right, that is, if I was interested. But I wasn't going to marry in a family my big brother had already married into. Forget culture; new ground was always better, and, besides, I was not going to think about marriage until, perhaps, after eight or so years. So, no, thank you, no marriage thoughts here at all. But Maiguru was saying, "Talk to him nicely; he'll take care of you one day."

"Fine!" Vonai said, sticking out that tip of her tongue towards me.

She then went silent, for a while, looked at nothing, like she had turned herself off. She looked beautiful that way. I was going to paint a portrait of her beauty in my mind, for later use in a possible novel, but she bounced back with, "So do you still do that church thing?"

I hesitated for a while, but yes, I was still a proud practitioner of the Word, junior deacon, if she wanted to know the specifics.

"*Inga, VaMu*deacon,"[6] she said, pretending to be pious. "So where do you go to church here?"

"I happen to attend the Glen View branch," I said. "Way bigger than Mototi."

"*Inga!* We shall join that church too then," she said, then refocused her attention on Maiguru. "You know with time, Auntie, given all the money I'm making, I will go back to school."

"That would be a good thing," said Maiguru. "You know Babamunini here is in Form Five?"

"He is..." Not a question, not an expression of surprise. "Be careful now, Babamunini. Don't get too educated for me!" Vonai said. "I can deal with the deacon thing, but too much education, no-o-o."

I did not get a chance to respond because Mukoma entered the room. He had been out fixing someone's electric stove in the neighbourhood. At first, he looked exhausted but when he saw Vonai, his eyes lit and he said, "Look, who's here finally?" He reached over and hugged Vonai, who proudly rested in his arms. He held her close, and with a low voice said, "Looking all grown and ripe."

Vonai chuckled. Maiguru rolled her eyes, and shifted on the couch to open room for Mukoma to sit, but he and Vonai remained glued together. He was, culturally, as good as her husband, was more entitled to her than I was. Come on, the man had paid bride price for the girl's aunt. As much as there were limits to what he could do, what could stop him to say to the girl's father one day that he had put together some substantial amount to pay the bride price of a new woman and that he was interested in this beauty here? Maiguru and I watched them, waiting for the right moment to greet Mukoma.

"You two stop it now so we can find where to look," said Maiguru, with a voice more playful than it was annoyed.

Mukoma disengaged and I greeted him. Vonai fixed her top, which had slid down. I looked away, but my eyes met Maiguru's, which also

---

6   *Inga, VaMu*deacon - lucky you, honourable deacon

averted to Vonai, and I followed them, and ended up just looking at Vonai fixing herself. There was no harm in looking with empathy; she obviously needed help in many things about this life. She was young, that's why, but as Maiguru had said, she should be careful in the presence of her boss's ex-husband.

Mukoma sat on the same side as Vonai. Normal dialogue resumed, dominated by Vonai and Mukoma who seemed to be in a contest of playful words. She could talk! You wouldn't think that she was only sixteen. The subject matter did not return to the issue we had been discussing before Mukoma arrived. She became a different person altogether, asking questions about life in Harare, about Mukoma, about what working with electricity was like, and once in a while asking me about A-Level education and whether I was planning to attend a local university or a South African one like one of her uncles had done.

She had taken over the stove and cooked us an early dinner. Mukoma told her that he was happy to see her, so happy that after we had finished eating they played a game in which she ended up on his lap and he finally got to pinch what was culturally his. All the while, I sat there trying to read *Black Sunlight* by Dambudzo Marechera, but it was not the sex scenes in the story that caused a little stir in me, but the way these two played, with Vonai shrieking, half-exposing herself when she jumped and said to Mukoma, "Babamukuru, don't ever do that again!" He was allowed to pinch her chest; even Maiguru didn't seem to mind. That's what *babamukurus*[7] did to *maininis*,[8] right?

But when she shrieked, he knelt on the floor and asked for her forgiveness, an apology she accepted by kissing him slightly on the cheek, to which Maiguru said, "You two are taking this *chiramu*[9] too far." She looked serious at first, her lips quivering, but ended up saying she was just joking when Mukoma knelt in front of her too and

---

7   *babamukurus* - (plural) husbands of the elder sisters to the speaker
8   *maininis* - (plural) younger sisters of the wife to the speaker
9   *chiramu* - a relationship in which the niece regards her aunt's husband's younger brother as her 'junior' husband in a Shona cultural sense.

117

apologised. It was fun to watch. I felt a bit inadequate because I started to think that, perhaps, Mukoma was this playful with Vonai because I had not entertained her, as I should have done. But our church didn't allow all the pinching of breasts and the grabbing of waists, so I guess he was welcome to entertain her on my behalf.

After another two hours she said she was leaving.

"You are not staying the night?" asked Mukoma. "I'll divorce you; what type of wife are you?"

She explained that she had to hurry before her family returned from Seke, where their church was located.

"I thought this was your family," said Mukoma. "You have not come to stay?"

"She works for the family," Maiguru cut in with a sense of finality.

"Ah, that's good," said Mukoma, who didn't seem interested in knowing the details. "Just make sure you remember to come back here soon."

"Of course, husband, this is where I belong," she said.

Maiguru rolled her eyes and said, "She is only free on Sundays."

"Sundays are okay," said Mukoma. "She should visit us often. Harare is too big and can swallow you if you don't connect with others." Mukoma had assumed his advice-giving tone. "And be careful out there."

"You know I will," Vonai said.

"I'm not joking," said Mukoma.

"I know. See you again on Sunday."

I got up to find my shoes because I was going to walk her to the bus stop — that I could do. It wouldn't be appropriate to let Mukoma do it. But he surprised me by getting his shoes too.

"Let Babamunini walk her," Maiguru said. "The two have a lot to talk about."

"I wasn't going too far," Mukoma said, but he listened and sat down.

Vonai hugged him tightly again. Then she leaned to hug Maiguru, a brief tease of a hug, and to me she said, "I will give you yours at the buses."

On the way, we did not talk at first. I was hoping she would say something, but she was quiet. I couldn't talk about books to her, and generally I didn't have much to discuss with people in general except books or church matters. So she had to be the one to initiate a conversation; otherwise I didn't mind walking in silence the whole way. But still, she did not say anything. She seemed ponderous and nervous, which turned me tongue-tied too. On and on, we walked, but I started growing more uncomfortable and guilty. At least, I had to say something, as the older person and as a man, ask her about her favourite books, or about what she was planning to do when she grew up, that is, when she returned to school and pursued her education as she had told Maiguru earlier. I realised then that this was the first time I had been alone with her, and I started to be aware of the fact that I was walking with a girl from Mazvihwa this far away from home. It was not every day that a thing like this happened, walking with a homegirl. And those who saw me could tell that I was walking with a girl, a beautiful one at that.

A car zoomed by, spraying gravel on our shoes. She jumped and gasped, as if she was about to curse the driver, but she then went silent again and walked faster. Was she really waiting for me to speak first? I scratched my head, only because my scalp really itched. Of course, I was supposed to be the one to initiate dialogue. I was, as Maiguru had pointed out, a potential future husband to this girl… no, not that, but because as a junior deacon I was used to initiating dialogue, to offer advice to members of the congregation, even those who were older.

"Were you serious about coming with me to church next Sunday?" I said, surprising myself with the steadiness of my voice.

"Of course!" she said, livening up again. "I don't want to be alone. You know I don't work on Sundays. I've the whole house to myself and I'm bored to death."

"Well then, I will make sure I come by so that we can go together," I said, wishing to withdraw my offer right away, but she smiled and looked directly at me with a measure of honesty in her intentions. In the light, her smile was dazzling, but I didn't want to act like I saw it. Instead, I said, "You'll like it; they dance better than back home."

"I like the sound of that, Babamunini," she said, twisting her waist to demonstrate a dance. It wouldn't have qualified as the dance one did at our church, but I appreciated that she had attempted a dance. It wouldn't be bad to be seen arriving with her at church the following Sunday.

"After the service we could do other things," she said. "I want someone to take me to movies and...," she tailed off as if she was unsure whether she should talk about movies to me. Although I had never been to the movies, I nodded to encourage her to talk about them.

"Have you ever gone to the movies in town?" she asked.

"Yes, once or twice, a long time ago," I said and even tried to remember what movie I had seen, but ending up trying to imagine how the inside of a cinema looked. "I don't go often because I have no one to go with usually, and the studies sometimes steal my time, you know."

"No worries now, Babamunini; if you like, you can always take me to the movies. I saw *Waiting to Exhale* in Gweru with that man I told you about."

"That's a good movie," I said. I had read the novel, so I could say one or two things about it. She didn't have to know that I had only read the book.

"I will go with you to check the church out, since you said they dance better," she said, "but I can't have that stuff of men trying to do the prophecy thing on me. I am just coming because of you." She paused. "After church you can always come with me to the house." She raised her voice to a pitch of excitement. "Did I tell you I have my own room?"

I hesitated to answer because, for the first time, I suspected that she was trying to seduce me, but she was too young for me. Well, maybe not, since I was only nineteen, but she was definitely not my type, if I had any type. Books were a major qualification, if she wanted to get my attention. For now, I had to answer her question, so I said, "Your own room? That's great." Then for some reason I started picturing us in that room after church, with her crawling towards me or something. I pictured myself getting tempted but, of course, ending up overpowering temptation. Then I started feeling guilty for letting my thoughts wander inappropriately like this.

"You can get to shower after all that church dust. Then we go to town to do something." It all sounded unbelievable what she was saying and, of course, there was no need to take her seriously.

"Right," I said. "You have the whole house to yourself on Sundays?" I asked.

"All of it, *mufunge*,"[10] she said, leaning towards me, but I knew that didn't mean anything, so I moved away.

"Sweetie," I said, moving back closer to her. "Can you give me the address? I can take you to church and to the movies and to the house."

"House first, to clean up," she said, which made sense. "People get dirty at your church, and I don't mind it, but I have to shower after that."

"We don't get too dirty there. We sit on the grass, and most people bring mats and chairs."

She pouted and said, "Still."

"But you are quite right though, people still get dirty because the dancing gets serious."

When we arrived at the bus station, I gave her a pen and paper to write the address. When I saw the details, I realised that the house was in a walking distance to the Glen View church. So that meant I would get in an emergency taxi to Makomva Shopping Centre and then walk the rest of the way to the house. We would then walk to Bonongwe Forest, where the church gathered under a *muchakata*[11] tree near the

---

10   *mufunge* - just imagine, or can you believe it?
11   *muchakata* - a big indigenous tree in Zimbabwe whose fruits are edible. It provides good shade for many people.

Mukuvisi River, which was convenient for baptism, in case she would end up getting converted. She liked the way everything sounded, and I was going to ask her more questions about her employers, but her bus arrived and she said, "I guess that's it for now then, Babamunini. I really enjoyed your company." Somehow she really knew how to say things in a way no other Mazvihwa girl would have.

I was going to hug her only, making sure I did not grope for her or come in contact with her chest, but I don't know what got into us. I don't know who initiated it first, but our lips kissed for a second, then she turned quickly, and while entering the bus, shouted, "Bye and later!" As the bus thundered away, I stood there confused by what, at nineteen, was my first kiss and a sin. Walking away from the bus terminus, I focused on thinking about plans for next Sunday. I looked forward to bringing a new member to the church.

Back home I found Mukoma waiting for me outside.

"She is a lot fun, isn't she?" he said.

"Just so-so," I said. "She wants to come with me to the church."

He flashed his eyes in surprise. "She doesn't seem like a church kind," he said, chewing his lips. "Just be careful. She comes off as someone you cannot trust, and remember, you can't mess up on your studies." He paused to peer at me, to make sure I was listening. "You know why you are here, right? Here in the city?"

"I wouldn't do anything with her. She's just a baby," I said, hoping he wanted to hear this. Mukoma was just like a father to me, and I was not free to discuss certain matters with him, especially those pertaining to girls.

"There's nothing called a baby, once a woman reaches that age. Remember, your Maiguru was only fifteen when we got married." He looked at the door, perhaps to check that Maiguru was not listening. "Even then, she was mature enough to know what she was doing." He paused, as if to allow me to respond, but, although I saw his point now, regarding how old Maiguru had been when they got married, and how old Vonai was, I didn't have anything to add or subtract to what he was saying. I coughed instead, and he resumed, "I'm not saying don't take her to church, just don't get crazy ideas into your head. You're a bookman and she, what… she's just a…you know!"

I laughed to show that I knew, but I didn't. Then his face became serious.

"If you mess this one up, I won't hesitate to take care of you myself," he said. "If you think because you are nineteen you can do what you want here, you will have to face me man to man." He leaned closer and whispered, "Besides, if I were you I would stay away from her. Your Maiguru doesn't mind another woman joining her. We have been talking for a while about how we need someone here who can bear children."

I opened my eyes wider.

"If all goes as I am planning, there is a chance that before the end of the year, I may add to the size of our family," he said, now speaking with his normal voice. "You understand what that is, of course. Doing what Baba Taru did."

Baba Taru, our half-brother, was a husband to three sisters whose ages ranged from seventeen to twenty-five. The sisters' father was so impressed by his son-in-law that he wanted him to be the only man who took care of his daughters. He had given him a big discount on the bride price of the youngest sister.

I looked at Mukoma but my mind was not there anymore, and I wasn't sure what it was focusing on. Behind Mukoma, the door opened and Maiguru filled the entrance.

"Are you two coming in or what?" she said. "I made some tea."

Mukoma turned and said, "Give us a second."

She closed the door slowly, her face lingering in the disappearing opening and when the door closed, Mukoma said, "Stick to church and books."

"That's what I do best," I said. I could feel a knot in my throat.

Smiling, he said, "As for the plans, I will let you know the details. For now, make sure none of those good-for-nothing prophets at your church try to prophesy my little wife into marriage with them."

"I will watch her for you," I said, the whole idea tickling me. I wanted to laugh.

"That's good," he said, and then with a more serious tone, because the door had opened again, he added, "I can't just watch as you ruin your life."

I nodded vigorously, watching Maiguru, who was grinning in the doorway.

"Let's get in," Mukoma said, walking towards the door. "The lady of the house cannot take it anymore."

I followed him, and for the first time contemplated extending my leg to trip him. But we entered the house, sat at the table like gentlemen, and drank tea in silence.

The First Night

Mukoma said his second wife was too new to be taken to the village to meet the senior wife, Maiguru MaMoyo, so he left her in the city with me. I was not going home since a prophet had warned me against visiting the village before writing my A-Level examinations. He said the witches would feast on me and I may not end up writing the examinations, and if they allowed me to write them, I would definitely fail. Mukoma wanted me to stay in Harare as doing so meant I would watch his wife while he was gone. "What's good about all this," he said, "is that you also get to study the whole weekend, day and night. Don't let her make you turn off the light if you feel like studying all night."

I nodded to show my appreciation.

"In fact, I want you to read all night," he said. "That will make your job of watching her easier." He paused. "Besides, with examinations around the corner, you don't have a reason to sleep anyway."

I told him I would use the time wisely.

He smiled and, with a low voice, said, "Don't let her go out of your sight." He nodded directly in the direction of the door to show that he was referring to his wife who was cooking inside.

"Are you sure you understand this whole situation?" he asked. And when I hesitated, he added, "Of you staying here while I go home to see your other *maiguru*, of you keeping your eyes open."

"Staying up all night will be easy to do," I said.

"I know it will be easy," he said. "Because if you let her slip, I will hold you responsible."

Hold me responsible? Was he drunk already? But I reassured him that I understood what I was supposed to do.

Later, when the wife found out that she wasn't going to the village with her husband, she beamed, especially when he told her she would have my company. She had already told me a few times that she respected my commitment to school, so I knew I would be able to study without her distracting me. But I doubted that if she were to decide to go out at night, I would be able to say anything to her or to Mukoma after he returned from the village. She would definitely have found a way of helping me keep my mouth shut; perhaps I could make a little pocket money from the whole arrangement. Or, maybe, this was another of Mukoma's jokes.

On the first night, I didn't study. Mukoma's new wife and I lay down early, she on the bed, I on the sofa. But I couldn't sleep, no matter how hard I tried. To my surprise, I was thinking about her the whole time. She probably was thinking about me too, judging by how she kept tossing from one edge of the bed to the other. Through a hole in my blanket, I saw that she was looking in my direction, but she didn't seem to notice that I could see her.

I knew she was naked in that bed. Just before she got into it, when I was about to walk out of the room to give her some privacy, she had said, "Babamunini, just cover your head, or close your eyes." I had covered myself with a blanket, my eyes closed too because I could have seen her through the thin blanket. Her blouse crackled as she pulled it off, and soon, as I was fighting a thought about breasts broken free, the bed springs squealed as she buried herself under the covers.

"You can look now," she said, "and keep the light on if you want to read."

"I'm taking a break tonight," I said, the dryness of my voice surprising me.

"I would too," she said softly — seductively — but it was too soon to tell why her voice had suddenly gone soft. "What's he going to do? Come back in the middle of the night and tell you to read?" She laughed and said, "*Izvozvi handiti*[12] he is in the arms of his stupid wife?"

---

12   *Izvozvi handiti* - Right now, as a we speak, isn't it that...

This surprised and confused me. I hadn't thought she would care about Mukoma being with his wife, considering she hadn't minded stealing him from her. She had agreed to share the husband with her. The only difference was that she knew about the existence of the other wife, while Maiguru didn't know about her. And the reason this marriage had to remain a secret, as Mukoma had told me, was that the new wife was too new to be introduced to Maiguru. Another reason why her statement confused me is that she was no stranger to the arms of many men, having been a prostitute not too long ago.

I didn't say anything. Under no circumstances would I discuss Maiguru with her. In fact, I made it clear, by my long silence, that I didn't appreciate what she had just said or implied. She had no right to be jealous. She had no right to be lying on that bed.

She remained silent too; lay looking at me with one eye because her pillow pushed into the left eye, closing it. She looked relaxed though, as if she really enjoyed my company.

Looking back at her eye, I said, "My decision not to read has nothing to do with Mukoma but, as you know, all work and no play..."

"Made Sivindo a fool; I know," she said, breaking into a laugh. That wasn't the saying, but well...what could I say?

I turned the lights off, told her good night and lay down. I tried to fall asleep, but my mind kept focusing on her and I didn't know why. I closed my eyes, but I knew she was still peering at me in the darkness. Soon my eyes would adjust to the darkness and I would see her eye staring at me.

I shouldn't be thinking about her like this, I thought, this is my brother's wife. These thoughts were not appropriate for a man of my stature. They were a sin, the worst kind. Over and over again, we preached that thoughts about fornication amount to fornication. The woman sleeping on a bed, a former prostitute, was trying hard to share my brother with his wife. Well, that didn't matter, Mukoma considered her his second wife. She was his second wife, which is why she was sleeping in his bed.

I closed my eyes tight to block the evil images that were invading my brain. I blocked the images with swirls of darkness, yet I kept thinking about prostitutes. She lay restless on my brother's bed. Once a prostitute always a prostitute; I had heard this statement enough times to believe it now; and it bothered me. This was temptation: why had I been left alone with this woman?

I was lying in the same room with a woman who only recently left Kubatana Beer Hall with men, going to their dark rooms, or creeping into Bonongwe forest to do all kinds of dirty things. Hungry hands tearing off nylon and cotton... I pictured her returning to the beer hall to be picked again by another man, or groups of men at the same time, with two or more women... I had read somewhere that some people did it in groups, and prostitutes were likely not to mind orgies (one word I discovered accidentally, reading about the spread of pornography in South Africa), as long as they were paid. I had once overheard Mukoma telling his friend that he had done it with three women at once, in the same bed. And he was close to doing that again, if Maiguru MaMoyo would come back with him. For a moment, I started to think of Mukoma as a lucky man, who would be living or lying between two women, or would it be one of the women lying between he and the other woman?

****

Maybe the bus Mukoma had taken that morning was finally crunching the gravel road in Mhototi as it swung to a stop at the Mupani stop... I pictured Mukoma alighting and hugging Maiguru, who had been waiting for him for hours, then planting one of those brief town-people kisses he had trained her to receive... Then I wasn't thinking about those kisses in Mhototi anymore, but back here in Glen View, where hungry hands of strange men groped for what they had paid

128

for… female bodies defiled…And to imagine that a body like this could one day settle down and be married by my brother…

She shifted again and I bit my lower lip to make the pain clear my dirty thoughts. No room for temptation here and no need to invite Mukoma's fury. He had asked me to watch, not to munch her. She could sleep there in her nakedness, and I would stay on my sofa, thinking about clean thoughts. If she asked me to join her on the bed I would just pretend not to have heard her and start snoring. But if she insisted, saying, "Come on Babamunini, you are as good as my husband too", I would join her but lie with my back to her, fighting temptation — *get thee behind me, Satan*; then maybe she would intensify her temptation by letting her hand…, but I wasn't that kind of person. I was a deacon in a fast-growing church. The prophets would feast on me come Sunday once they knew what I had been thinking about. At the thought of prophets my mind cleared.

Her breath came out softly, an even, musical rhythm. Her presence was growing heavier by the minute, as if it was a weight I was carrying on my shoulders. I lay there motionless, listening; then I remembered what she had asked me once: "So does the church allow you to do anything at all?"

"Anything?" I had said, pretending not to know what she was talking about but wondering where she got the courage to ask me such a dirty question.

"You know anything…something," she said, pointing on the ground…well, not on the ground. Mukoma was in the room, and she wanted the question to be understood only by me. I had been shocked by what I understood, and how I saw a flash of a naked body heaving; then I blinked the sin away and said, "Oh, the church? I play an important role in it."

She acknowledged my response with a smile that allowed just enough front teeth to peep through pinched lips. That was the first time I noticed her beauty, enhanced by the gap in her front teeth. I didn't know then that tooth gaps were ugly in other cultures. She had stood there as nothing else but pure woman, empathetic-looking, as if she saw the injustice in my platonic existence. But then I had stiffened and found myself hating her for implying that there was something wrong with my status; nothing could stop me from following my Lord, not even her star-like smile, not her eyes that were full of promise, eyes like little secrets.

"You're blessed," she had said after heaving a sigh. "Young still, but already saving souls."

"He'll outgrow it one day," Mukoma had said, "but it's good for him now, so he can finish school without distractions." Some of his explanations were beginning to embarrass me, and I felt I needed to speak for myself more but, again, Mukoma was Mukoma; he could tell people whatever he wanted about me and there was nothing I could do about it.

He was like a father to me. The only problem was that I knew with absolute certainty that I would never outgrow my church commitment; I knew that, based on his terms of interpretation, it might worsen, which to me meant strengthen. But his new wife didn't have to know everything.

On another day, when she and I were alone, she asked if I had a girlfriend, or if I knew what to have a girlfriend meant. It was a strange question considering my age, but I understood the basis of her curiosity. And I told her "no" to the first part of the question and gave a strong "yes" to the second. Come on, who didn't know what to have a girlfriend meant? You just went out there and found yourself a girlfriend, easy as that.

"Just asking," she said. "These things are important, and I ask because I care."

Those words of hers — *I ask because I care* — sometimes made me wish I was in Mukoma's shoes. But the right thing was to show her that the Word was more important than women, who would come later

130

according to His will. And as for being in Mukoma's shoes, no, those shoes were too big for me.

"Just trying my best to avoid the things of the flesh," I said and she winked at me.

"You realise though that once in a while the earth must shake and the skies must rumble?" I liked how she said it, and I even began to wonder how she had gone into prostitution if she was that intelligent with language. Or, maybe, she had ended in prostitution because she was that smart, smart to figure out that being there was the best option she had? That had to be it; and now, look, she had found herself a husband who was someone else's husband. Yes, that took a degree of intelligence and great planning.

"Is that from a book?" I said, in earnest. "What you just said about the earth shaking and what-not."

"A book?" She started laughing. "You forget books are written by people?" I joined her in the laughter.

Mukoma found us laughing, and as he entered the room, said, "There you go you two. You are getting along well. Good!" He always wanted to make sure that I got along with his women, whether that woman was his wife or some weekend fling.

She was asleep now. Her breathing had grown heavier and was threatening to develop into snores. The two of us here, much like when I used to sleep in the same hut with Maiguru in the village. But I was little then, and Maiguru slept in her clothes all the time. But this one here was just *musvo*[13]…with only those sheets clinging to her. How lucky they were…but I wanted to think about something cleaner. The red edges of the Bible or something else… a woman sleeping on the bed, but covered in white or red church robes, a prayerful Zion woman, prophesying in sleep. But my thoughts peeled the folds of those robes and exposed the nakedness. The sheets and blankets were probably laughing at me now, thinking, *just get up here, man, and explore.*

---

13   *musvo* - stark naked

I let my mind drift to Mazvihwa again, following the route Mukoma had taken that morning. When he got on the Masvingo bus at Mbare, he slid open his window and shouted, "Remember what I told you, *mupfana!*"[14] I had nodded and waved, and, as the bus left, he waved a goodbye to his new wife.

When we were walking back to the emergency taxi station for Glen View, she asked me what Mukoma had been telling me. She asked in a lazy way, as if she didn't care really what he had told me, as if she was just asking for the sake of asking.

"Oh, you know, about studying," I lied.

"He really wants you to succeed," she said, walking so close to me that her hips bumped against my waist. But what man's waist would not want that to happen?

"He does, yeah," I said, walking faster.

"The funny thing is you are the kind that doesn't need to be pushed. If he had my cousin Ruvengo for a younger brother he would go nuts."

"How come?" I asked, uninterested.

"My uncle has tried everything, from beating to starving, but the boy just can't get it. All he likes is playing soccer, and now he's into girls, and he's only fourteen!" She started laughing, and I tried to imagine what kind of girl she had been at fourteen.

"We all come in different packages," I said.

****

By now, Mukoma was in Mhototi, having arrived before sunset. If he wasn't at a beer gathering, as there were always plenty of those on weekends, or at the small beer hall at Vhazhure Township, he was at home with Maiguru in their bedroom. Or, if they had not made it all the way to the bedroom hut, they were lying on the kitchen floor, hungry hands fumbling in the dark. Maiguru's hands, most likely, her earth-abused hands. I really was not supposed to think about that, but I had to

---

14   *Mupfana* - a Ndebele word for younger brother or just someone younger than the
       speaker.

keep my mind far away from this room where the woman breathed heavily on the bed. Maiguru was probably just as naked as this woman here. Greedy hands groping. Couldn't blame her, after three months of drought that's what people in the village called it, the drought of women whose husbands worked in the city and returned home every three or four months.

And Mukoma was there now, doing what I, if I wasn't such a coward, should be doing here. Why lie here like a log if I was supposed to just say, "Are you asleep?" She could say something like, "No, I'm not. Are you?" I could then laugh, and she would laugh too, laugh so hard that she would sit up, forgetting that she was naked, and let the blankets fall, then continue to laugh, as I would be doing—louder, almost choking on that laughter, coughing, but laughing still, getting up to turn the lights on. Then, with her standing in the middle of the floor, I would continue laughing, trying to make her realise that she didn't have anything on, but maybe she would tell me she didn't care about my role in church, about what Mukoma would say; and with my stare fixed on her, I would let temptation take its course.

She was snoring now, piercing my peace. I should already be dreaming too since there was no way we could do anything, not with what would happen to us later once Mukoma found out: fists splitting skulls, rags of clothes thrown out of the door, a walk into the darkness, and the impenetrable strangeness of Harare, walking into the mouth of doom..., and later, the raging pit of fire...

Suppose something could try to happen, which I doubted, the age difference would not permit. She had told me that although she looked young, she was thirty-two, almost fifteen years my senior. She was ancient. But... Mukoma had said that she hadn't given birth yet, which meant that things were still intact...Despite, of course, the many men...

My thoughts were illegal. The Sunday sermon, about reaping what's between the legs of other people's wives... death glaring you in the eye. No more of this nonsense between...my...; this couch. The village:

the fumbling….Mukoma in Mhototi heaving; Maiguru MaMoyo coiling…..
And this woman here: seriously, when did these two do it? I never heard
them at night; did they wait when I was outside, or away at church or school?
In fact, in all his dealings with this or that woman he brought to our room,
Mukoma never allowed me to catch him in the act. Never. Or did I sleep
like a log? I doubt that; the slightest whisper could rouse me from sleep.

"You can turn on the lights if you want to read." Her voice, husky with
sleep, startled me, drew me out of encroaching sleep. I sat up, and then lay
down again.

"I can't read tonight," I said. And I shook my head and pinched my
thighs together and covered myself with the blanket.

"That's right, but it sounds like you are not falling asleep," she said.

"Oh, I will soon," I said, forcing a yawn.

She turned over, and I wondered if her body was still fully covered by the
blanket. I closed my eyes and imagined holy hands being laid on an ailing
soul, but I started thinking of her turning into something disgusting, a roach,
a caterpillar, or even a slug. Thinking of her this way would soften me and I
would be able to fall asleep.

"Try to sleep then," she said. "Remember tomorrow you're going with
me to town."

"I know."

I looked through the hole in my blanket, but I couldn't see anything, so I
slowly peeled the blanket off my face. In the semi-darkness I saw that she
was still fully covered. I sighed inaudibly. She began coughing, her body
bouncing up and down. The war between my legs started to rebuild, and I
bit my lower lip hard to let my mind focus on the pain. Once again, I ended
up thinking about rotten things streaming in like rats, a stench in the pit of my
mind. I curled, closed my eyes and relaxed. The fire within started to die
down, and I knew soon I would drift into sleep, but I couldn't sleep too
deeply since I also had to watch her in case she tried to creep out of the
room.

"I can't sleep, Babamunini," she said, startling me again.

I pretended not to have heard her.

"I said I can't sleep," she said, a little louder, like a complaint.

But I was sound asleep, so she left me alone. I heard the springs of the bed creak, then the thud of feet on the floor, and I held my breath. Then I heard her walk towards the door. I lifted a corner of my blanket. She had wrapped herself with a sheet. She opened the door and closed it, but didn't lock it, so I knew that she was only going to the toilet. Usually, if you listened hard you could hear her, but it would be inappropriate to try to hear her now. I covered myself fully before she returned so she wouldn't think I had been awake. But then I wanted to wake up with a start, for her to think that she had just disturbed me.

The door opened and closed softly. She tiptoed towards the bed and climbed with the least noise, the springs not screaming under her weight. Shortly after, as I held my breath, she started to snore and I exhaled. As I listened to her snoring and the constant buzz of the Glen View night, I fought the revolution between my legs. I whispered another short prayer and concentrated on clean thoughts: in two weeks our church was going to Domboshava to fast for the rains, a weekend *masowe*[15] characterised by non-stop singing and rib-snapping prayer. I was planning to go. We were also planning a trip to NeNguwo, to open a new branch; we would stay there the whole weekend, cementing the relationship between our branch and theirs. I liked visiting new churches far away, and especially in the rural areas. The girls there were mellow and always showed interest when a young man from the city talked to them. Once, in Madziwa, I almost got myself a supple Korekore girl, but then I found out that one of our prophets had already talked to her. And when he talked to your girl, you were better off moving on, looking elsewhere. You were then better off contemplating spending some time with any woman you met in the city, you could even think of a prostitute and…her snoring was ceasing, and I wondered what she was dreaming about, if she was dreaming.

---

15   *masowe* - prayers conducted in the wilderness or in open places away from home by members of some Apostolic churches.

Soon the revolution died. And I was in Runde River in Mhototi, chasing some kind of creature. Then I was being chased. But when I stopped running, I was in Glen View again, this time sitting in a mansion. I stood up though, when I heard a falling sound. I entered one of the bedrooms and found thousands of ants streaming out of the base of the bed. The ants became roaches, and I was running through the house opening cabinets but not finding bleach. Then I was in a big bed, sitting on the edges and spitting out little insects, which turned into vultures that stabbed the wooden floor with their beaks, advancing towards me, and when I was spitting another mouthful of maggots, a light behind me dissolved the vultures. And her sharp scream roused me from sleep, but, drenched in sweat. At first I didn't know where I was.

I looked around in the darkness and realised I was still in the room, on the sofa, and she was still in bed, but braying. I sprang up and dove for the switch. She was on top of the blankets, in a naked coil, her mouth wide open. What was she trying to do? What type of trick was this? As I wondered whether I should come closer to the bed or look away, I noticed that the rest of her body looked lighter than her face or legs. She lay with her back to me, but her head was shaking vigorously. I moved closer to see what was going on. Maybe she was dreaming. I didn't want her to wake up and find me looking at her, so I started tiptoeing backwards to my sofa.

She broke into another scream and her body heaved and turned. The front area poured into my direction and I felt a strange dizziness, which cleared when she bared her teeth and emitted a deadly groan. Everything shook — thighs, shoulders, her massive breasts, her lips, but her eyes were closed, pinched together in pain. I didn't know what this was. I didn't know what to do. Perhaps turn the lights off? But her bellowing deepened and I swung around to look. Her eyes looked at me with their whites. My heart started pounding.

I had to do something. Help her stop screaming at least.

"Are you okay?" I asked, as I stepped forward, then back. I could not — it was not appropriate — to get too close to her. Are you okay? My voice was shaking. Her body went limp, and I ignored some of the sounds it began emitting. I didn't know whether to touch her, to turn her flat on her back and feel her heartbeat. There was a lot of her I could not just touch without crossing boundaries. Perhaps I should pray for her. Her body seemed to be in pain, and trusting that it was not a kind of gimmick she was using to seduce me, I could go straight for those first aid steps I had learned at school. I edged closer to the bed, stamping my foot on the floor to see if the noise would make her stir. She didn't move. A sudden chill gripped me and I started sweating. If something happened to her, if she died, I would be in trouble. All this, whatever it was, would be blamed on me.

She lay still, as I bent over to access her chest, avoiding focusing on her breasts, which poured to her sides. As I was about to slip my hand under one of them to feel her heartbeat, she quivered and let out another scream. I jumped and staggered backwards. She struggled to sit up, and her eyes opened, met mine, and dimmed again. Her wrists were twisted, and she turned on her side, assuming the same position she had been in when her scream woke me up. I was dreaming. No, she was dreaming. No one was dreaming. I waited for her to stir again and she didn't, but I could see she was still breathing, peacefully as if she had resettled into sleep. I was about to turn off the light and go back to my sofa when she rolled over again to face me. Her body was jerking harder now, and her left hand, whose fingers were twisted, was trying to tell me something with an up-and-down movement, as if it was trying to show me something on the floor. I even looked on the floor but saw nothing, then I realised that it was moving in response to the tension of the upper part of her body. I looked at her face again, hoping that she would tell me what to do.

I started walking towards the door, but stopped in my tracks because I didn't know where I was going. Perhaps this was the real temptation, a test, a trial, but what had I done to deserve it? Satan's paws were in everything to do with the arrangement, right from Mukoma telling me to watch her, which I was doing right now, but how could I have prepared for a watch of this magnitude? But a man of the word can face anything, you don't allow fear, do something *mu*deacon.[16] Pray for her, pray for yourself. Cast out demons. I could sprinkle holy water on her face. I had not used it in days, so at first I couldn't find it. It was in my jacket pocket in the wardrobe, which is where I should have looked in the first place. With the little bottle of holy water, I was ready to face whatever this was. No demons had power in my presence. I stiffened, drew a thick draft of air through the mouth and released through the nose. I could feel a spiritual grip that squeezed out all the fear or hesitancy in me. I advanced, held her head in place and closed my eyes. I lay my right hand, which had the water bottle, on her forehead and, shaking my head, whispered prayer: *"Help your murandakadzi;[17] give her power to fight the demons enyika."[18]* Suddenly, an invisible power flung me away from her, and when I opened my eyes I was still standing where I had been, but what touched her forehead was not my hand, but the butt end of the tiny water bottle. She was shaking her head as if a spirit was about to seize her. Bring it on Satan. I resumed praying, in English, the closest I ever got to speaking in tongues.

She struggled like one possessed, producing a shattering, throaty sound that didn't scare me in any way. My prayer became louder and with my eyes still closed, I opened the bottle and sprinkled some water. She bobbed up, then I heard her relax. I opened my eyes, which met hers. I backed up to put away my bottle. I kept my eyes, on her forehead. Then she realised that she was naked and curled. I looked away. I should have covered her with a blanket before I started working on her. I was about to apologise when she broke into another scream.

---

16   *mu*deacon - a deacon
17   *murandakadzi* - woman servant
18   *enyika* - of this world

138

If I let her continue groaning and lowing, people in the other rooms would wonder what was going on and come knock on the door. I didn't want to be found looking at a naked woman. I thought of covering her mouth with a cloth, and while the other hand lay on her head as I prayed for the sudden end of whatever had seized her again, she started foaming at the mouth, her head twisted to the side and eyes now closed tight. I knelt in front of the bed, lay my hands on her shoulders and uttered another prayer, and all I managed to let out was a weak "Go away. Go away." The prayer was interrupted by another sharp scream, as if she had been stabbed. I managed to cover her with a blanket but her groans grew, coming out rapidly. I helped her to a sitting position. When she was almost sitting upright, she jerked forward like someone about to vomit, pushing me so hard I staggered back to the couch, but I got up again to fight the forces of Satan. What I saw as I moved back to the bed made my skin crawl and, for the first time, I was afraid. I considered bolting out of the room. Her face looked like a screaming skeleton. As I was about to search for my Bible, she twisted again vigorously and before I could jump towards the bed to prevent her from falling, she fell hard on the floor and went quiet and flat.

I stood over her and started shaking. My throat was dry, and a wave of dizziness caught me, but I shook it off. I took a jug of water and sprayed some of it on her. This water was not holy but it was cold enough to wake a rock. At first she did not move, and I was worried, then, aware that every moment of mine was becoming useless, I poured more water on her, and she jerked up and said, "Hey! Stop that!"

She sat up quickly, like one coming from a bad dream. She looked around and then at herself. Our eyes met and she gave a weak smile, grabbed a blanket and covered herself. She sat there for a while, her shoulders drawn forward like she was cold, which she was, looked on the floor. I stood there waiting for an explanation; otherwise I would wake up tomorrow thinking I had had a very bad dream.

She lay down on the bed and as she covered herself snug with the covers, she said, "Turn off the lights, Babamunini, and try to sleep."

I didn't react.

"Or you can study for the rest of the night if you want." She then sank deeper into the bed, covered her head and began to snore… I turned off the lights, avoided any further thoughts about this and went back to my sofa.

****

In the morning, I was roused from sleep by the squeal of the door. She was walking in from the sunlight.

"Rise and shine!" she said, as she raised her arms and I noticed that she had a grocery bag in her left hand.

"Good morning," I said, avoiding eye contact with her, but she smiled and said, "You sleep like a log. I even tried to wake you up so you would run to the stores. Breakfast will be ready soon."

"I'm sorry. I was just too tired I think," I said. She looked normal, which disturbed me a little.

"I don't blame you," she said softly, but after a short pause she raised her voice and added, "Long night. I should have warned you."

I hesitated, my eyes focused on her feet. I opened my mouth to say something, maybe tell her that, whatever it was, could not be blamed on anyone, but I closed my mouth before I said anything. A pure case of words being stubborn for reasons only they knew.

"I understand. You don't have to explain anything, Babamunini." She looked at the door as if she was afraid someone may walk in. "As far as we are concerned, nothing happened last night."

"But I could almost say something did," I said, gaining eye contact with her.

For a moment she didn't say anything, looked confused even. I started to feel bad. I was about to explain that she was right, nothing had happened, but she said, "I am sorry to let you see that. I was thinking that once I got married it would stop."

"Oh," I said. "What was it?"

"You tell me you don't know? Even better then - you might as well say you saw nothing." She looked at the bed for a while. "I can tell it hasn't happened in almost a year, and your brother has never seen it." She put the grocery bags in the kitchen corner of the room. Then she sat and fixed her skirt. "So it can be our little secret that he doesn't get to know yet."

"Exactly what I was thinking, if you say he doesn't know yet," I said.

"Really?" she said, standing up. "That means a lot to me, Babamunini."

She stood up and walked to the stove, and holding up an egg, said, "Scrambled or fried?"

"Scrambled, please," I mumbled.

As she got to work, I folded my blankets, and arranged them on the sofa like cushions; then I found a book and went outside to read, but I just looked at the words without comprehending anything. My eyes were not moving across the page, but just pierced through the fence of words as I tried to think of how many of her other secrets I would be prepared to keep.

A Long Night

As soon as Mukoma returned from work, even before he jumped into the shower as he normally did, he called me into our room and told me that he was going to marry a second wife. He said it was official, our family was finally growing. I didn't know what to say, but I nodded while my mind wandered to the village, where his wife, Maiguru MaMoyo, lived alone several months out of the year. I tried to imagine what she could be doing at the very moment her marriage was being impacted. Was she at the river, watering the garden, or at home working in her little vegetable garden?

"It's happening, *mfana,*" he said. "And you know I have always wanted this to happen."

I didn't know that I knew that he had always wanted this to happen. I had thought all this time that he didn't care about marrying more than one wife. I didn't even think the fact that his wife could not bear children bothered him enough to want to marry a second wife. But now I liked that he was asking me for my opinion, something he rarely did. Indeed, this was a sign that he thought I was now grown, and maybe that was why he was now opening a new chapter of growth for our family.

He was looking at me expectantly; I had to give him my opinion.

"It's time something like this happened," I said. "Being big is a good thing."

"You got that right," he said, sitting down. "Your words show wisdom."

I knew I wasn't supposed to show surprise, given my new wisdom, but I did, not because the news was unusual, but because he had decided to tell me first before bringing the woman home. I was no longer just his little brother who stayed in the periphery of his city forays. I smiled widely, making sure that he saw my face.

142

"Do you remember what I always tell you about these things?" he said and waited for me to answer.

I could have told him that I remembered, but then he told me many things and, in this instance, I didn't know which thing was relevant, so I said, "You have told me many great things. And I appreciate you telling me many of these things. Not many young men my age have big brothers who are like a father to them." I could even feel the grittiness of my own words, so when he didn't look impressed by my response I wasn't surprised. I felt bad for failing to remember the one thing expected of me to tell him that I remembered. "You are great to me," I said, feeling the dryness of my mouth and wondering why I was acting this way. He raised his hand to stop me from saying more. It was as if words were letting me down.

"I want you to remember that even if I bring a second, third or fourth wife, your Maiguru is the one closest to here." He brought his hand to his heart. "Do you understand?"

"That makes great sense," I said.

"It doesn't have to make sense to you," he said, his voice rising. "What's important is that you understand it."

I understood him, and I showed this by grinning, but that didn't mean that I agreed with him. My opinion wouldn't matter anyway, since I was required to focus on books, go to college and come back as a useful member to our family and of society... then I would begin my marriages. Until then, I would just have to watch him marry his wives, nod my understanding when needed, shake hands with him in congratulations. I knew too that by saying wife, he was actually talking about a prostitute, with the hope, as I had known many to do, that she would be tamed into a housewife, stuck or glued to one man for the rest of her life.

"So you really are bringing a second wife?" I asked, just to take the conversation back to its original focus.

He nodded rapidly, then he said, "But you know the only place in here is for your Maiguru." His hand was on his chest again. But he didn't have to plead his case with me, really. He was eighteen years my senior; he could do whatever he wanted without caring a tiny bit about what I thought, but to keep the dialogue going, I said, "I know Maiguru is the only one."

"I didn't say the only one. She's the most important, not the only one." His voice had become rough. "She's the most important, not the only one. Big difference there."

"Yes, huge," I said, nodding. I put away the book I had been reading, *King Lear,* and gave him my full attention.

Mukoma chewed his lower lip, the way he always did when something he liked was about to happen. I liked that he was happy about this decision, but I began to wonder how Maiguru would react to all this.

I could never complain because Mukoma had allowed me to live in the city to study for my O-Level examinations without the disturbances of cattle herding and field work back home. I felt then that I had no choice but to show interest in what he was telling me. In other words, I had alredy begun to understand that I owed him a lot, and supporting his decision-making was one tiny step in my paying back.

"Don't worry about any of these women ever treating you badly," he said. He had lowered his voice, acquiring a softness I wasn't familiar with. "They all have to know that you're the reason I work hard every day."

I felt a wave of excitement and told him thank you. I loved his consistency on this issue. From the time I had turned twelve, he had told me, repeatedly, that no woman in his life would replace my position of importance to him. "One day, you will understand these things, as long as you remember that your duty now is to work hard for our family's future."

He pulled out a cigarette pack from his shirt pocket, looked at it for a moment, and then put it back into the pocket. "So my plan is to bring her here in two weeks," he said in a relaxed voice. I felt like an equal to him.

"So Maiguru is coming here in two weeks?" I said. I knew that didn't make sense, but it was the best I could do, for Maiguru didn't know that her future was being affected.

"What do you mean?" he asked, frowning. In fact, he opened his eyes wider as if to get a better view of me.

"Which Maiguru is coming?" I asked. "The regular Maiguru from the village?"

He opened his mouth, closed it again and shook his head. He probably thought I was joking, but I was not.

He leaned forward and said, "What's wrong with your ears today, Fati? Didn't I say 'new woman' right now?" He clicked his tongue to show his irritation. "Are the books beginning to mess up your head? He-e? Do we need to end this school thing right now and send you back to the village?"

I shook my head. I couldn't afford to go back to the village. He could bring whatever woman he wanted, it was his business.

I pushed *King Lear* away with my foot, images of a king in the storm flashing in my mind, and said, "Oh, so it's the new Maiguru coming tomorrow. That's good news!"

"A brand new sister-in-law for you," he said. "What do you think?"

I grinned. I knew my face showed genuine interest. He smiled back.

"The city kind," he said. "Gorgeous. You'll see when she comes."

"City women are beautiful," I said. I knew he would appreciate my comment. I was old enough to engage in talk of women with him. Judging by how he responded, he must have realised that I was more than just a book-consuming machine.

"You don't worry about women," he said. "Yours is a life of books for now." He stood up to signal the end of our dialogue.

I was perfectly happy with my book life, and I wanted more of it. In the city I could find any book I wanted. I was already a member of three libraries: British Council, where I read British literature and newspapers; the United States Information Services, where I spent at least an hour watching news about the war in Iraq, but I always borrowed good books on my way out - Toni Morrison, William Faulkner, Richard Wright; and the Russian Library, where I read Maxim Gorky, Anton Chekhov and Nikolai Gogol, reading them just for their names at first, so that at school I would tell Jabulani and Tonderai, my friends, about the new literary names I had discovered. Pronouncing those Russian authors' names made one sound well-read. Book hunting was my pastime and I didn't want to risk finding myself in the village again. So fine then, Mukoma's role was to search for women, and mine was to search for books. This new woman was somebody for Mukoma to while up time with in the city. I really didn't believe that he was serious about making her his second wife. But, as if to affirm his seriousness, he said, "This is going to be the only woman, besides your Maiguru, I'm going to keep in the long-term."

I nodded and smiled at the prospect of someone brand new coming to join us. Perhaps, she had a beautiful young sister. Who knows, I might also start mixing books with other little bits of what would constitute my total future. I was sure Mukoma wouldn't mind much one step at a time.

****

He brought her within a week, on Thursday, June 30, 1988. I entered the date in a notebook in which I had begun to keep records of important events in Mukoma's life, which I knew, in one way or another, were important in my life as well. Were I a writer, which I was to some extent, I would have started writing our family memoir, a family primarily consisting of Mukoma and I, but writing about Mukoma would

146

automatically mean writing about the women in his life... and, with this situation, whatever woman would enter my life ... whenever I would get married. But in the notebook I noted the arrival of this new woman, whom I didn't yet think of as my sister-in-law. Maiguru didn't compare to this city woman, a tall, light-complexioned, ready-with-a-smile woman who greeted me like she had met me somewhere already. I noticed it all, the lightness of her hands, both in colour and weight, so light you could see the veins inside, sharp contrast to Mukoma's complexion, which was a sooty black kind, the deep, dense presence of a tall man standing beside his very light-almost-white woman. The village would talk about her, and they would praise him. These were the women everyone back home wanted to see. She was lighter than Maiguru, who was lighter than Mukoma's first wife, Mai Benjy. I just couldn't help imagining how light Mukoma's next wife would be if he stayed on this course, but he had already mentioned frequently that he would never cross racial lines.

She gave me an intense greeting full of gasps and sighs that impressed Mukoma, who stood nearby smiling and nodding. His look was the kind that assumed I was proud of him for bringing home such a beautiful woman, so beautiful for a moment I forgave the fact that he had met her in the beer hall, that she had been, and could still be, a prostitute.

"That's the one," Mukoma said, pointing at her with his chin, and widening his grin.

I extended my hand to shake hers, but I was a bit hesitant, and she noticed.

"I have heard that you're a genius," she said. "You're in Form four, right?"

That touched my heart, the word 'genius.' "I am almost done," I said with a pleasant voice. "As you can see, I am preparing for the November examinations." They both nodded, but I could tell they were waiting to hear more, so I added, "You found me reading *The Sound & the Fury*."

"By James Hadley Chase," she said, confidently. I had somehow expected her not to know the author, but I hadn't expected to hear such a wild guess. She widened her smile, and I could have made her believe she was right, but I didn't want to be responsible for letting ignorance spread like HIV/AIDS.

"No, it's not by Chase," I said loudly and paused to see her reaction, but she only gave a brief laugh. That forced me to be kind, to say, "It's by William Faulkner, an American author."

"Same thing," she said, looking at Mukoma, who nodded in agreement.

"I used to read Hadley Chase too," I said.

"That's good," said the woman. "I'm new but I can tell you, Babamunini, that I'm proud of you."

Her "Babamunini" was not as natural as Maiguru MaMoyo's, but it was…sweet; it was new, different.

"Can I go to the shops to get you a Coke or something?" I said, desiring a moment by myself to review my life up to this point and to think about the change that was about to happen.

"No, Babamunini, read your books," she said, leaning forward, spilling cleavage.

What a woman, quite a keeper. I widened my painful grin and opened room for her to sit by me on the couch. She made as if she was going to accept the offer, but swung and sat on the bed with Mukoma. They both faced me, and somehow I felt a certain power, seeing them looking at me like that.

"If you think that I don't know about Maiguru in the village," she said, "I do. I like my position of junior wife, and I can't wait to meet my senior." She looked at Mukoma sideways; then broke into a laugh, which I found pointless, but a laugh is a laugh.

I surprised Mukoma with a congratulatory handshake. And that's what I wanted - to surprise him with a gesture of manhood, to show him I understood fully what was happening.

148

We settled down to the business of the evening: I resumed studying, Mukoma played Tuku music, and the woman, occasionally twisting her body in tune to that beat, deep-fried some catfish on our one-burner stove, every now and then fanning the smell with a folded newspaper. She located the utensils and condiments easily, and told me to relax and read in peace.

Hallelujah!

When she left the room, Mukoma whispered, "She thinks she might be pregnant." He allowed me to nod in wonder. "And as you know, I have been trying all these years with your Maiguru." I continued to nod, tilting my face to show empathy and understanding. Especially understanding, because a lot of that was needed in this house. He needed to be understood, I needed to be understood, Maiguru in this village needed to be understood, and as for this new woman, did she too expect people to understand why she had decided to join a married man? When Mukoma mentioned that word, pregnant, you would have thought something sweet, something more than savoury, was dissolving in his mouth.

He and Maiguru had been married for eleven years but there had not been a child and, by now, everyone in the village knew it was Maiguru's fault. Mukoma had already had a baby with his ex-wife, Mai Benjy, whom he impregnated at eighteen, when she was sixteen, so the villagers had the proof they needed for Mukoma's fertility. Besides, there were stories to go with Maiguru's infertility, and the popular one was that her jealous uncle had blocked her womb by tying the skull of a chameleon in a blood-soaked cloth and hanging it on the top-most branch of a *mutsviri* tree. Some said that the curse could have been reversible had not a bolt of lightning struck and fried the charm. He had managed somehow to steal a strand of Maiguru's hair which he used to tie the cloth around the charm. It was a family affair— the blocking, or locking of Maiguru's womb. And it couldn't be blamed on Mukoma. Maiguru would still not have been able to conceive even if she had married someone else. This story, and several variations, always came up when Mukoma and Maiguru visited *n'angas,* who always promised that their solutions would reverse the curse. But that reverse never happened. Year after year they tried, and year after year no baby came. No matter how many *n'angas* they visited, none could reverse this curse, and it became clear that she would never be able to conceive a baby. I had watched the problem wrinkling her face, transforming her from the always-laughing woman my brother had married to a stiff-lipped, eye-squinting field slave. She battered the soil like it knew where babies hid before they decided to be born.

Then, after seeing how hard she worked on the family farm, the village changed its story: now Maiguru was a valuable wife who gave her husband harvests of maize and millet. The village said, "She may not be blessed with children, but look how her husband's granaries are always choking with grain. He should keep this one no matter what." So Mukoma had kept her, had even argued that he did not care about other women. Marriage was not always about children, he said, and he shocked the village by announcing that he loved her. Rumours spread about how Maiguru had bewitched him, made him forget what was important, and how he was doomed to age without a child to call his own, since Mai Benjy had escaped with their son to Tanzania in 1972 and no one had heard from her ever since.

Five years into Mukoma and Maiguru's marriage, the village started predicting that Mukoma was headed for polygamy, but I had always doubted the possibility of this one. I had overheard Mukoma tell his friend Jakove, who had two wives, that he could not deal with two or more women under one roof. Mukoma had said he would keep one wife - Maiguru - in the village home, and, as a man, he might see other women in the city. And that he had done. In the five months I had lived with him in Glen View, he had brought several prostitutes home, but not one he had announced as a new wife.

150

And now this? At least, he thought she, the woman now cooking and dancing in our room, was pregnant. A niece or nephew for me was not a bad idea at all. I even smiled at the prospect of spoiling a child who may grow to look up to me. That's what, should anyone ask, was in it for me.

She crept back into the room, a smile on her face, looking at me with stunning, big eyes. I turned to Mukoma who had grown unusually quiet. He nodded his acknowledgment of something, perhaps my pride, which must have been apparent on my face. The Tuku cassette that had been playing clicked as it switched to the other side, but Mukoma removed it and put Leonard Dembo's *Shiri Yakangwara*.[1] Even I was going to dance to this one, but I brought back my attention to books since the lady of the house had told me to relax.

In all my surprising excitement, I had not thought about what was to follow after her visit and how the marriage was going to work. It was, therefore, with great shock that I listened to Mukoma's announcement that she had come to stay.

"After dinner, be ready to come with us to her place," Mukoma said. "We're better off doing everything tonight."

"Her place?" I asked, but the look on Mukoma's face caused me to say, "I'm always ready."

"I need two strong men to help me move," the woman said, with smiles like little lightning flashes on her face. "In case he didn't tell you, I'm joining you all."

My stomach rumbled so loudly that they both heard it. I shifted on the sofa and leaned forward. "So you're here to stay?" I asked the new woman directly.

"I thought I told you before, or that it would be obvious," said Mukoma, but I really wasn't talking to him, so I kept looking at the woman sitting on our bed like she was Maiguru.

---

1   *Shiri Yakangwara* - a clever bird

"You knew this already, young man!" said Mukoma, with a rising voice.

Of course, I knew. What was I thinking?

The new woman looked around the room and said, "You have a nice home here." She looked at me. "You have kept it very clean."

What was she talking about? Anyone could keep a house clean, whether she noticed or not, but I decided to thank her for the compliment.

"I told you he would make you proud," Mukoma enthused.

"And it's a big room, I mean, *very* big," she said, her voice thinning, and the lower lip dangling with… something…pride, perhaps.

"It's big and ready for you, woman," said Mukoma as the woman spluttered into laughter. I, too, broke into a laugh to hide my chagrin. Calm came into the room, and I prepared to follow along as Mukoma led the way, each to his role, as we had always done.

That night we went to her shack in Glen View 3 to collect her belongings and brought them to our room. We brought two suitcases of clothes since she told us that her sister was going to collect her remaining belongings. I was glad that two suitcases were all we had to carry since we had walked.

Soon after we returned, Mukoma updated the landlord regarding our new living arrangements to make sure we were not breaking the contract. We found him sitting outside in front of the house, smoking and drinking alone.

"So what are you going to do with the young man?" asked the landlord, who everyone called Carpenter, although that was not his line of work.

"The room is big," said Mukoma. "You know how these things work."

Carpenter laughed. "But suppose we had an extra room, would you consider renting it for him?"

"He'll be fine. We'll figure something for now."

But I would not be fine, because even as Mukoma declined Carpenter's offer, it became clear to me that although there was a sofa which I would use as my bed, an era of discomfort had just begun.

Although I had always considered the day I arrived in Harare as the day that marked a significant change in my life, the arrival of Mukoma's new wife to share our room with us marked the real change but it was too soon that night to tell if it was change for the good or not.

I slept on the sofa and Mukoma and the new woman used the bed on the opposite side of the room. They allowed me to keep the light on when I studied. During examination time, or nights before a test, I could easily read all night while they slept. And when Mukoma woke up to go to the toilet he would mumble something like, "Ah, you are still reading? Good." But not all was good.

I decided I would not invite my friends and schoolmates to my home. If we needed to meet for studying, we had to go to the library or to their homes. Also, there was Bonongwe, a forest outside of Glen View 1 where all sorts of people met. Lovers went there to picnic and sometimes ended up doing what the world was safer not seeing. Apostolic Faith and Zion Christians went there to fast. Prostitutes and their clients crowded the area too. Often, they were seen transacting between the huge granite outcrops of the forest. Then there were students who favoured to work in the company of nature. At least, that's how I looked at it, and I got a better understanding of Thomas Hardy there. The forest became my main library, and once I introduced my friends to it, they stopped suggesting my home as a possible venue. But each time I was there, I would not stop to think that the prostitutes we saw were the same kind of people with whom my brother's new wife compared, that perhaps she had haunted this place as well in broad daylight.

The day the new woman confirmed to me that she was pregnant, Mukoma was still at work, and I was alone with her in the room. We were busy laughing about something she had said regarding new babies when we heard a knock on the door—a light, patient knock. Since I sat closest to the door, I stood up and opened it but shut it immediately, hoping that my eyes had lied to me. I reopened the door, and there she was, Maiguru, smiling, actually laughing actually.

"Babamunini, you are still very funny," she said. "Let me in, *please*."

She handed me her small suitcase and started climbing the two stairs at the entrance. I opened the door wider to expose the new woman, and for Maiguru to see that I was not alone.

She saw alright. And still she walked in, past the woman like she was not there, to the bed. She sat on the bed, her eyes scanning the room, looking at the new displays on the wall, female things hanging on a makeshift drying line between the wardrobe and the opposite wall. Then she looked at me, finally her mouth still twitching with a smile and her eyes telling me something that I couldn't interpret.

The new woman joined me on the sofa, sitting so close I could easily have guessed that Maiguru thought maybe she was my girlfriend. When the two women remained quiet, I didn't know anymore if I was expected to do anything, so I got my book and started looking for a page to read.

"Babamunini, are you going to introduce us or what?" said the new woman. I ignored her. I actually found the page I had stopped reading.

"Babamunini," the new woman called again, bringing her face closer to my ear. I felt her warm breath and the unbearable softness of her side. "I'm talking to you. Introduce us."

I decided to surprise her: "Introduce yourselves to each other, ladies." Then I sat back and watched.

The two wives of my brother sat up straight and looked at me like they thought I was crazy.

"Yes, Babamunini, she is right. Introduce us," said my own Maiguru. "You know what to do."

I looked at her for a sign that maybe she had not really meant what she had asked me to do. But she twisted her lips and waited. The new woman looked at me sideways, rather seductively. They were both waiting for me to act.

154

So I did.

"Maiguru, meet *maiguru*," I said, pointing from Maiguru to the new woman, whom I hadn't been able to call Maiguru yet.

There was silence in the room. They looked, not at each other, but somewhere - the senior wife at the ceiling and the junior, the new *maiguru* looked out through the window; then they both turned and looked at me. I shrugged and stood up, to escape their stares. Mukoma would have to take care of this himself.

"Where do you think you are going?" the new woman asked.

"Outside. I will be right back." I then opened the door. And guess who was standing outside. Mukoma, his ear tilted towards the door. When he saw me, he backed up and started just dying with laughter, his shoulders jerking up with the impact of the laughter.

"You did good, *mfana*," he said. He then entered the room, holding another of Maiguru's small suitcases. He put the suitcase down and sat on the bed. The new woman joined them on the bed, sitting on the other side of Mukoma.

"I thought he was going to cry! Ha! Ha! Ha!" Maiguru MaMoyo said, choking from her own laughter.

"You should have s-s-seen him sh-sh...shaking; his eyes wide open like he saw a ghost! He! He! He!" Mukoma's new wife said, her face deformed by laughter.

But Mukoma's laughter died to a grin, and he looked at me. I sat on the sofa and listened.

"You did fine, young man," Mukoma said; then he turned to Maiguru and added, "Didn't he do fine?"

"He tried," said Maiguru.

The new wife nodded in agreement.

"But you two got to meet finally, although you almost killed my younger brother with shock," Mukoma said, wiping his hands, which had been labouring all day.

"Yes, we met. We were made to meet," said the new woman. "But we had not started official greetings." She then knelt on the floor, facing Maiguru, and started clapping theatrically. "How do you do?" she said.

Maiguru did not kneel, but she clapped, while intoning, "I breathe if you breathe too."

"We breathe and kick with life," said the new wife, pointing at her belly.

Maiguru forced a smile, much like something was biting her where she could not reach, and said, "That's what we want to hear."

When I asked Mukoma how his day had been I managed to fit in a "You got me today."

"I just wanted to jolt you a bit. They knew she was coming today." He paused to allow his women to nod and cough out brief laughs. "But you passed the test; you are now a real man."

I didn't know exactly what test I had passed, but, with an examination coming in a few months, I might as well get used to the idea of passing tests. Thus, I thanked Mukoma for the compliment, and picked up my book from the floor, excused myself, not to be rude or anything, and went outside to meet King Lear and his daughters.

That evening we went to eat at Makomva restaurant. Mukoma said it was a night to celebrate, and since it was a Friday, I didn't have much reading to do. So we stayed at Makomva until eleven. On our way back home, we hired a taxi. As soon as we entered the room, the new woman said, "So he sleeps with us?"

"No, he sleeps downstairs."

"Seriously, I mean, where's he going to sleep? And what do you mean by downstairs?"

"I mean downstairs, woman!" Mukoma barked, stiffened.

"Just explain something here," the new woman said. "This is a room in a one-level house, so I don't get it."

"You don't have to get anything, just understand it, you hear me?" said Mukoma, pointing at her with a quivering finger.

156

"I'm serious though. Does that matter?" She looked at him with an expression of disbelief. "When you made this arrangement of your wife visiting now, did it ever occur to you that we would find ourselves in this situation?"

"I am not just visiting," said Maiguru, who looked at me and whispered, "What does this woman mean by visiting?"

I shrugged and looked away. Mukoma lit a cigarette, pulled at it and sent a cloud of smoke towards me. Maiguru sat expressionless, but her eyes rested on the new woman, who shook from side to side, slowly. My eyes stung because of the cigarette smoke. The new woman had made a good point. It was time Mukoma realised that I was not a child anymore. At seventeen, I could be married, like Obert back in Mazvihwa. His junior wife's question was my question as well. Did he care about how I felt at all?

But again, this was Mukoma, the real man. How many men from Mazvihwa just said to their younger brothers, "Come, leave the cattle, come to the city and go to school and learn?" Not many. Some reversed their offers mid-way, afraid that the younger brother would excel and become more successful than they were. On the day I left the village, even mother reminded me to go to the city and mind my business. "Just chase books," she had said, "and don't look too much into the affairs of your brother. Listen to him; he is like your father."

The new woman shook her head more vigorously, and an expression of worry registered on Maiguru's face. Mukoma threw the stub of his cigarette on the floor and crushed it with his shoe.

"He will sleep downstairs," he said, in a more composed voice.

The new woman let out a loud laugh.

"I don't see anything funny," Mukoma said. "Does anyone see anything funny?" He looked at Maiguru and then at me, but we did not say anything.

"I can't help it," said the new woman. "He's in Form Four! You think he'll agree to this plan of yours?"

"Ask him," said Mukoma, pointing at me with his chin.

The wife looked at me, noticed something on my face, and said, "You know what, never mind. I'm not going to waste my time." She looked at her hands whose fingers were shaking. "He's your younger brother. None of my uncle's sons would tolerate nonsense like this."

"Listen woman!" said Mukoma, rising and resuming his seat. "What I do with him is none of your business. And who asked for your opinion anyway?"

The new woman leaned forward, titled her face to gain eye contact with the other woman in the room, but Maiguru averted her eyes and looked away. The new woman sighed and reclined against a pillow.

Mukoma assumed the air of authority I was accustomed to; then he addressed me directly: "All this is temporary. The bed is high enough for you to crawl under there and sleep comfortably. You will not even need a mat; just one blanket on the floor and another to cover yourself with."

I nodded. It all sounded doable.

Maiguru coughed, and then she said, "I slept under a bed when I lived with my uncle in Bulawayo. He called it downstairs too. I did that for a whole year."

I nodded again.

"Many people do that," said Mukoma. "You are old enough to know it, and educated enough to know what's important for your future."

I kept nodding.

"It's surprising that you say many people do that," the new woman cut in. "Not any that I know of."

No one paid attention to her. I pretended I hadn't heard her when I said, "If it's temporary, it's doable."

There was silence. Then I saw the look on Mukoma that I had always dreaded.

"And if it wasn't temporary what would you do?" he asked.

I opened my mouth…closed it, as I felt the muscles of my stomach tighten. But yes, what could I do? Tell him I wanted to go back to the rural areas? Or, maybe say…what?

158

"I asked you a question, Marechera!" he shouted, standing up and towering over me.

"Not now, *Baba B*.[2] Please not now," said Maiguru, standing up to restrain him from getting dangerously closer to me. But she had just made a big mistake.

Mukoma swung around, raised a fist and as it was descending towards her face, the new woman and I sprung up and held that arm like a log on our shoulders. Mukoma struggled to loosen himself from our grip, but came to stand still, gave a rapid sigh and sat down. We let him cool down, and when he had, he gave a brief speech.

"Listen, all of you! You think this is easy for me?" he said. "I'm trying my best here. Can someone see that?"

We sat looking at him, listening.

"You are all here because of me." He scanned us with his eyes, as if he was inspecting his crops. "Educated or not, you all report to me."

We listened.

"So this is how things are going to go." He pulled out another cigarette, but did not light it. "You two women will live together in peace. You two women will respect this young man. You shall let him study in peace, even if it means he will keep the light on all night. Understand?"

His two wives seemed to understand, but they did not have a chance to vocalise it since he continued, "As for you, young man, we are a family emerging from poverty. For now, while we emerge, we may have to do this. As I always tell you, concentrate on books and I concentrate on what?"

"On work," I said, although my instinct was to say women. "And on making sure our name grows and..."

"You know," he said, finally lighting the cigarette. "So you'll sleep downstairs. You can read all you want, even if you want to keep the light on all night, but when your bedtime comes, go down there."

---

2   *Baba B* - Father of B

I peered under the bed. There was a lot of room down there for a person or two.

"You can't continue to sleep on the couch anymore. It's appropriate and respectful that in the new situation, you sleep under the bed. You see my point?"

"Yes, this will work for me," I said, avoiding eye contact with the new woman.

"Does anyone have any questions?" Mukoma asked, looking at his new wife.

There were no questions. The discussion in the room changed to other things.

We heard some stories about the new wife's childhood, and Maiguru talked about a baboon that had been captured in our neighbour's field in the village, and how the neighbour had decided to domesticate it.

"Why would anyone want to domesticate a baboon?" Mukoma asked, collapsing with laughter. His new wife was just dying, and as for Maiguru, she had tears in her eyes.

I saw Maiguru's tears building into larger balls that began sliding down her cheeks. When she saw me staring, she looked down and suddenly covered her face with her hands, but Mukoma and the new woman, their faces advancing towards each other, did not hear the sobs that had begun to shake Maiguru's shoulders. I sank deeper into the couch, opened my book, and waited for the beginning of a very long night.

The Soldier Lodger

I returned home and found Mukoma fighting with the back-room lodger, a soldier married to a prostitute. Maiguru and Sisi, the maid, stood near the front door, watching. I quickly checked to see if Mukoma was not being hurt and saw that he had pinned the soldier's head on the floor and was hammering his spine with fists. I smiled and proceeded to my room.

I changed out of my work-clothes into a comfortable T-shirt and some sweat pants, since I was going to do my routine jog in a few hours. I wasn't even going to try and think about the fight, to attach any importance to it because Mukoma would always be Mukoma, but I heard a thud from the living room. Still, I resisted the urge to find out which fighter had fallen, avoided the temptation of ending up watching the fight altogether. Soon, Mukoma would be done with the soldier and I would find out from Maiguru or Sisi what had caused the fight.

To avoid going back into that room, I started arranging the clothes in my wardrobe and, satisfied, I looked around and noticed that my bookshelf needed serious alphabetising, so I got down to work, humming as I did so. I had just finished fixing Achebe to Dangarembga, and moving on to Faulkner, when I heard a loud groan from Mukoma, then another fall. I opened the door and found Maiguru and Sisi dancing…No, they were jumping, flailing arms, shouting at the two men to stop, but the fighters slammed into each other as if the women's screams fueled the fight. Sisi held her stomach and burst into tears and Maiguru shouted, "Stop it, *vanhuwe-e!*[1] Stop it, *hazvina kunaka!*"[2] I folded my arms across my chest and watched the dancers and the fighters.

---

1   *vanhuwe-e!* - Oh, you people!
2   *hazvina kunaka!* - This is not good!

This fight was going well, and I was quite satisfied with the way Mukoma threw punches, thinking, come on big brother; we have done this for decades. The soldier wasn't performing badly either, but I knew he would not last. No one ever lasted when fighting with Mukoma; we all knew that; and the soldier knew that, all the neighbours knew that, just as back home in Mhototi, everyone knew it.

Madhuveko, the other male lodger, who was actually my friend, materialised from his room and stood by my side, shivering with excitement and a stupid grin on his face. He, too, crossed his arms, in honour of Mukoma, no doubt, and watched the fight. No one ever saw the need to help Mukoma in moments like this, let alone try to stop him. The man knew how to take care of himself, and hated it when anyone tried to intervene. We watched him discipline the soldier, who must have done something bad to deserve this beating. What was he doing this far into the main house, anyway? His room was a separate shack Mukoma had built behind the house. It was separate from the main house for a reason, but here the soldier was, subjecting himself to potent blows from the man of the house. The designation 'man of the house', which I remembered the soldier scoffed at - could be part of the problem. The soldier had rented a room in the main house long before Mukoma started dating Maiguru, who was the house owner. Then, the soldier didn't even acknowledge Mukoma as the landlord. But Mukoma didn't know this because the soldier had only revealed it to me on the day I almost got into a fight with him. So while Madhuveko shivered and cheered on, and Maiguru and Sisi shouted what they were shouting, I took my mind away from the fight and focused on that day two years ago.

I had been reading a book in a sunlit spot at the back of the house when the soldier came out of his room and said, "Hello slave." He was funny like that, using random words, *et cetera,* but he had never called me slave before, so I didn't know how to respond, other than laugh, thinking that he had seen the pile of student papers on the ground and considered that I was slaving my weekend away. I always dreaded working on them and would always start by reading a book, and delay as much as possible the grading process. I could see then how someone might think I was a slave. I kept laughing, waiting to hear his laugh, but it didn't come. Then it occurred to me that he might be talking to another person, whom he considered a slave, so I stopped laughing and looked around.

The soldier said, "I am talking to you, homeless man."

Homeless man? Really? I thought about this for a while, considered the possibility of my being homeless, started thinking about how Mukoma and I had just recently started calling this house our home, and how I had dreaded the very thought of that once, thinking then that it didn't seem right that it was the woman, not the men, who owned the house. Rapid thoughts, but I hated trying to figure out things that could be clarified easily since the man who had spoken them was standing very close to where I was sitting. I said, "Homeless man? Me?" I even pointed at myself.

"You!" he said with a thicker voice. "You, you, you!" He was jabbing the air with his finger. "Or, maybe, you're not a man, judging by your living situation here."

Until that moment, I had always respected him for his service to our country — whatever he had done in the DRC or some other African country that had needed SADC or OAU military interference. I had always respected him for that, and for his age. He was at least five years my senior, but I was beginning to sense that we were entering the zone of disrespect. A faint dizziness of anger, some careless sense of confusion, started to creep in. I sat up and said, "How's the going, man?" I wanted to keep the encounter civil, but my voice had betrayed me, it had been too loud, rather careless, splintering in directions I didn't want it to go.

Instead of answering my greeting, he said, "You and your brother are a shame to all men." He had lowered his voice to a breathy, rapid whistle which showed me that he was getting angry.

A shame to all men. He had used this phrase before, talking about Mukoma and me, but back then we were just joking about the increasing trend of men living in houses owned by women. I had even agreed with him back then, with his idea that he thought that living in a woman's house was what was killing our country, that now women thought because they were beginning to own houses, and that they could easily cross the border and go to South Africa to sell and buy things, that they were in control; I had agreed with him on a matter that I didn't quite understand but I must have needed a friend, someone to discuss important topics with. I was nineteen then. But I had agreed with the soldier for the mere fact that the room he lived in actually belonged to his wife; she was the official lodger; he was the one who had moved in. But when Mukoma built the room behind the house, he gave them a new lease, so he was now the official lodger, and his wife, this former prostitute, had moved in with him. But on my encounter with him, Mukoma and I had not stayed long enough to earn the soldier's respect, as I would find out the further our confrontation went.

"It's already been a year and you still haven't found your own house," he said. "What do you have to say for yourself, nigger."

That caught me by surprise, his calling me that. I wanted to laugh even…it was pointless, this habit some people had of calling each other kaffirs, *mabhoyi*[3] and niggers, always getting the latter wrong, veering away from its black American neo-use of nigga, which was meant to strip the word of its original racist connotation. No, it was pointless, unfounded, irrelevant. But I shot back, and said, "*MaBhoyi*, you're funny."

"Ha ha ha, you calling me that?" He continued to laugh.

Nothing wrong with that, so I laughed too, and said, "But this is now our house."

"In your dreams, idiot!" he said, spitting.

---

3   *mabhoyi* - a derogatory term for black Africans, originally used by whites in colonial
        Zimbabwe.

Ah, this man. I sprung up and faced him. I could feel the tension in the air.

He frowned, probably because he couldn't believe my action. Then he moved towards me, jabbing the air with his finger and saying, "You don't stay in a woman's house and call yourselves men."

The frustrating thing about the encounter was that I had no quick way to know his motive, so even as I entertained his nonsense, I was trying to figure out why he was attacking me. I was trying to apply some critical thinking, the approach I always preached to my students.

He waited for me to say something, but he was better off not hearing what was on my mind regarding his wife, who, truly speaking, was the original renter. To use his terms, he was less of a man than either my brother or I. What was he doing living with a prostitute and calling her his wife? But I didn't want to sound mean, what he did with his life was none of my business.

"With you I can understand," he said, "because you're just a temporary teacher who makes peanuts." On this, he was right. "It's laughable, but your brother, he brags about his trade." My brother was an electrician, self-trained electrician. "Why is he still here, depending on a woman?" The soldier's finger still poked back and forth in my direction, and there was earnestness in the shape of his mouth as he uttered each word. He seemed to be educating rather than insulting me. Were it not for the contrast the finger-pointing made, I would have thought that he was sent on earth to teach me these things, to advise me, to let me in on the secret of women and the houses they owned.

"You're a useless bunch, worse than beggars," he said, moving closer.

"What are you even talking about, man?" I started shaking.

He responded with a smile.

We peered at each other like roosters ready to fight. I remember worrying that although I was taller than he was, I did not know how well I would fare if we actually ended up fighting. Who knew what he was capable of doing, and what skills he had? Perhaps he owned a gun, a grenade or some other weapon from the army; and worse, he might be like one of those soldiers who carried around army knives. On the thought of a knife, I moved back, but I was not going to run away.

He stopped advancing and started laughing, the excitement brightening his face. "I was just joking, man," he said, and then looked at my chair and books. "I see you're getting ready to mark papers, do your thing."

I let out a heavy sigh and said, "Please, don't joke like that again." My lips were now shaking, but I went back to my chair and pretended to be reading.

"No, you don't get it," he said. "I decide how I want to joke, and you're free to joke as you wish."

"Useless soldier!" I shouted, throwing my book on the ground and bursting out laughing.

"Now that's more like it," he said. "You and I can be great friends after all." Before I could respond, he retreated into his room and closed the door behind him.

From that day I avoided him. When we ran into each other, I would just nod my greeting, which he would return with a friendly bow. In fact, we had barely talked, although I knew that he talked respectfully, it seemed with Mukoma, whom he called "boss". No one would have guessed that a day would come when I would find him fighting with Mukoma. But here he was, holding his own. They wrestled and rolled on the floor like they had a whole century to bring this fight to fruition. The soldier began to shout obscenities like "Spineless man; useless son of a bitch," which infuriated Mukoma further. Maiguru and Sisi continued their dance, punctuating each landed blow with a crescendo in their wailing. Madhuveko and I stood, he chewing his lips and I jerking my head in response to the flight of fists.

The soldier broke free and punched Mukoma in the face. Mukoma stumbled backwards, but regained his balance, yet before he could raise

166

a fist, the soldier released a kick that disappeared between Mukoma's legs. Maiguru covered her face and twisted to the side like she was dodging a blow to her head. Mukoma didn't seem affected by the soldier's kick; in fact, he let out a brief laugh…no…a groan! because he doubled over and brought his hands to his crotch. Oh no!

I dashed closer to the fighters, my hands forming into fists, but I remembered I was not the kind to join a fight in the middle. I stepped back to continue watching from a respectful distance, but Madhuveko jumped up, forward, then back again and looked at me. Because I didn't understand what his jumping meant, I redirected my gaze to the fighters. Mukoma had repositioned himself, and was convulsing with anger. It was the look I knew very well, his body's signal of impending victory. "Any moment now," I whispered to Madhuveko. Our attention on the fighters, we ignored altogether the pleading gestures from Maiguru and the maid.

The soldier somersaulted and pushed Mukoma to the floor; then he pinned him down and started bashing his face with a half-open fist, using his knuckles to dig into the flesh. I had never seen this type of palm-knuckle fist, but it seemed to work because Mukoma appeared to be in pain. He struggled to free himself, but the soldier applied more of his - I could just think of them as - army tactics. I realised then that he might become the first person to beat the big man, so I leaned forward to get a better view, preparing myself to intervene when needed.

Madhuveko jumped forward again and beckoned me. I ignored him. I just wanted to see what else the soldier was going to do, what techniques I could learn. Madhuveko grabbed the soldier's shoulder, but he was donkey-kicked in the shin; the soldier could not afford to turn and face Madhuveko. He concentrated on Mukoma, head-butting him twice. I could see Mukoma's face swelling.

"Do something, Babamunini!" shrieked Maiguru. She was really beginning to irritate me. She even drew closer to me, wringing her hands.

"Please, please, please, this is too much and you are just standing there!" said the maid. I pretended not to have heard both of them. But Maiguru shouted, "Babamunini!"

I titled my head towards her. She looked like she was about to swallow me alive. "Wait just a minute, ladies," I addressed both Maiguru and the maid. They could leave the room if they didn't want to watch the fight.

Maiguru gave me another scalding look. I ignored her. If she knew Mukoma as well as I did, she wouldn't worry herself, or better yet, if she knew Mukoma as much as Maiguru MaMoyo in the village did, she would just sit back, relax, and watch the man do his work.

Madhuveko stood by my side again, laughing. No, I wasn't going to go down in history as having laughed at Mukoma being beaten by a soldier, but I could see why Madhuveko was laughing. It was the way the soldier seemed to be winning, releasing blows that reached Mukoma's face without resistance, but still, he was the one breathing heavier. Mukoma was letting the soldier beat him on purpose, maybe to let him exhaust himself first before he taught him a lesson. I had seen his technique enough times to know that sometimes he prolonged fights on purpose, giving his opponent false hope for victory.

Maiguru started shaking with anger. Our eyes met and she said, "What's wrong with you?"

"Who?" I said. "Me?"

"I cook *sadza* for you everyday but this is how you repay me?" She paused to catch her breath. "Isn't that your brother there being abused?"

Abused? I looked at the two men and saw no abuse. Even Mukoma turned and looked at his wife as if to tell her not to meddle in his business. He then turned back to the soldier, heaved up and toppled the soldier easily. The soldier fell on the floor with a thud. He tried to get up, but I was there within a second, pinning him down, and before I realised it, I fell on my back, seeing first the roof, then the fury of the soldier and Mukoma as they both descended on me. They kicked me out of the

168

way and I wriggled to safety. That's exactly what I had been trying to avoid. I looked at Maiguru, to be sure she had seen this, but she had left, had gone to their bedroom. Something told me she had gone to get her gun, but I shook the thought off as a silly result of watching too many western movies.

The two men charged at each other again. That's when the real fight began, as they exchanged chunks of fists like gifts. Mukoma threw a fist that sent the soldier reeling backwards, but the soldier shook his head, growled and charged forward like a bull. By the time he reached Mukoma, his arms were outstretched and, for a moment, I thought he was going to hug him. Mukoma kicked the soldier in the stomach and he staggered backwards. I jumped out of the way, but Madhuveko pushed me back in harm's way and said, "Do something. Beat the soldier!"

"You beat the soldier!"

But the fighters decided to take the matter to my room. Mukoma's kick that missed the soldier forced my door open. Mukoma stumbled forward with the impact of his own kick, and this gave the soldier the chance to push him forward into the room. The soldier followed and closed the door behind him and locked it from inside.

Maiguru came out of her bedroom when she heard my door slamming shut. We crowded at the door, listening; then Maiguru started knocking and calling Mukoma's name, who after a while groaned and shouted, "Go away!" This was followed by sounds of falling and breaking things. My wardrobe, my bookshelf, something was falling in there. They were destroying my room. I tried to say something to Maiguru but she waved me away and said, "Don't even." Madhuveko shook his head and, looking at Maiguru, said, "This is too much, I know."

"Leave now!" Maiguru said, pointing to the other door. "To your room!" Madhuveko bowed and entered his room quietly. He stuck his head out and, pointing at my room, said, "Things don't sound good in there."

I knocked on the door, now determined to go in and help demolish the soldier, but before I could turn the handle, the door flung open and Mukoma, wiping his hands on his pants, appeared in the entrance. His face was swollen, but I saw that his eyes, which now looked at me, burned with anger. Suddenly, I had the feeling that he was upset at me.

"That was some fight," I said. "Is he still in there?"

"Out of my sight!" he shouted and pushed me out of the way.

I regained balance and watched him walk past Maiguru and Sisi to the master bedroom. I peeped into my room and noticed that the soldier was not there anymore. I looked under the bed, behind the wardrobe, and when I was about to check inside the wardrobe, I turned to the window and noticed that it was open, curtains dancing in the breeze.

I checked the damage in the room. Except for the books strewn on the floor and my bed out of position, everything looked amazingly normal. Now, that's what I call clean fighting, I thought as I walked back into the living room. I was desperate to find out what had caused the fight.

The maid stood in the middle of the floor, looking at the roof, in supplication. Maiguru had already followed Mukoma into their bedroom. I moved closer to hear her and tilted my head to suggest that I wanted her to tell me what had happened but she gave me a dirty look and said, "Don't even think about it, coward." She then entered the kitchen and closed the door. I wanted to follow her there, but looking at the time, I knew she was going to start cooking and would not be able to tell me anything. In the master bedroom, Mukoma and Maiguru were arguing, but I could just make out fragments of what Maiguru was saying: "...who cares about what he tells people? Eviction?...Who said that? What other man?"

What had happened here? A fight smack in the middle of the day, between two men I had thought had no reason to fight, one a lodger - and a soldier - the other a landlord - and a civilian. Well, 'landlord' in quotation marks, but I didn't want to conclude that the soldier's attitude to our presence here, or our claimed status as landlords at the property of a woman who had become Mukoma's wife long after the soldier had begun to rent from her was the cause of the fight. I didn't want to think that there had been something between the soldier and Maiguru...he was younger and Maiguru had taste, so that was out of the question.

I sat down on the sofa and listened. The bedroom door swung open, and Mukoma came out, now in different clothes. I looked down, to avoid his eyes, then I heard him say, "When I come back I don't want to see you here, understand?" I looked up to see if he was talking to Maiguru. But he was looking - and pointing - at me. "Follow your friend, do whatever, but make sure both of you are gone when I return."

I opened my mouth, but before the words came out, Mukoma shot out of the house and slammed the door behind him. Maiguru rushed to the door, opened it, made as if she was about to follow, but turned around and slammed the door shut too, and entered the bedroom without turning to look at me. For the first time, I started to worry that there was really a big problem, and apparently whatever had happened might have something to do with me and my... friend. The soldier? Madhuveko?

I stood up, felt for my wallet, but before I made up my mind about what I wanted to do, I sat down again as if the sofa was a magnet, and I started thinking. Soon, Mukoma would arrive at the beer hall and join his friends. They would wonder what had happened to his face, and he would tell them about how he had disciplined the soldier, how he had then argued with his wife, and told his younger brother to vanish... But what wrong had I done? I leaned back and sank deeper in the couch and waited for either the kitchen or master bedroom door to open.

Mai Lily's Promise

As she had promised two years earlier, Mai Lily, the mother of Lily, bit Mukoma's thing behind Chinendoro Elementary School. Mukoma, anxious to find out about his daughter, had agreed to meet Mai Lily to schedule another meeting at which the daughter would be present. After the first meeting, Mukoma, Jakove, and I would go back to Kubatana Bar, while Mai Lily, who was a prostitute again, would return to a different bar. The meeting was not supposed to end the way it did.

Mukoma had asked Jakove and I to be present as witnesses, I with a notebook and pen to write down everything, Jakove with his pair of eyes. Meeting at night had been Mukoma's idea, for he did not want Mai Tari, his current wife, to know that he was meeting with a prostitute. Mai Lily was already there when we arrived. She stood with her hand against the fence, swinging her right foot impatiently. Mukoma slowed down, extended his arms sideways to block us and said, "Let me handle this, gentlemen." Then, he advanced slowly, like a stalker.

The meeting started surprisingly well. They asked each other about life after marriage, talked about the year's delayed rains, the likelihood of another drought, and so forth. Then the conversation settled back on their life after marriage, and I took out my notebook.

Their marriage, which I had seen as mere *mapoto* or cohabitation, had led to the birth of Lily. Although it had gone on for two years, there had been no sign that the arrangement would last, but Mukoma, who had always wanted a baby, had not doubted its necessity. His wife of thirteen years, Maiguru MaMoyo, could not bear children, so a woman with a bulging belly was not easy to resist, a woman he had already *fixed*, the word he used to describe impregnation, but even then, I had known that it was a non-marriage.

Mai Lily had arrived as Melody but left our family as Chenai, because she said we, the Shumba family, had stained her name. She had to change it for a new start, not as the Melody who had once retired into marriage with Mukoma, but as the Chenai who had emerged from nowhere to end that marriage when Mukoma suggested that Melody join the senior wife in Mhototi. The non-marriage ended with a moderate argument since Mukoma didn't want Glen View to witness another of his fights with Mai Lily, but still, there was no time to discuss co-parenting, so Lily was bundled with everything her mother owned and taken away. Mukoma told me that Shumba children had a way of coming back at the right time. This meeting then was the first sign that a Shumba daughter was about to return.

Mukoma had told us that by arranging to meet with the mother, he was being considerate, to work out a temporary arrangement with her because the Shumba family, now serviced by a new wife, was not quite ready to receive its daughter home permanently. "A temporary arrangement," said Mukoma, "if this whore has a bit of sense and civility in her." *Civility* being a word he now favoured, having followed a divorce case that had rocked not only Glen View, Glen Norah and Highfield, but all of Harare, all of Zimbabwe. Men in beer halls had talked about it, about how the whore had been corrupted by new laws that allowed women to cause havoc in the new families of their ex-husbands.

After Mai Lily left, Mukoma married Mai Tari, but his first wife had left him subsequently. Maiguru MaMoyo said she could not take it anymore, 'it' being her husband's endless search for babies. Mukoma had cried for the first time, not because of the arrival of the woman who would soon become Mai Tari, nor the falling of his grip on Mai Lily, but because Maiguru MaMoyo had always allowed him to sleep with other women. She had finally left him, and he cried for an hour; then he told me to tighten my belt because the Shumba family would change forever without its rural horse, who, although childless, had always kept our rural home full of grain, a home people pointed at and said, "That's the Shumba home there, where the wife works like a donkey." Some corrected the speaker by saying, "You mean a horse" because a wife was a horse if her husband worked in a major city like Harare, and a donkey if the man was jobless and stayed in the village too. Maiguru MaMoyo finally rose one day, rose like the sun or moon would, packed her clothes, all the grain, and returned to her home a kilometre away. When Mukoma went to the rural areas and asked her why she had left, she had not given him even a second of her time, so he cried again.

Mai Lily had left, so had Maiguru MaMoyo, two wives leaving - one springing to her feet and declaring her departure, and, a month later the other rising like the sun or the moon, leaving Mukoma with the woman who would become Mai Tari, whom he had met months before Mai Lily's departure. This new woman had no dreams of becoming either a rural horse or donkey because she had completely grown up in the city, and she was a reasonable woman who had allowed Mukoma to move in with her, even offering a room for his rural wife, an offer that triggered Maiguru MaMoyo's departure. Soon, Mukoma found solace in his new wife's pregnancy, and he forgot about Mai Lily and the daughter for a while.

Then out of the blue, Mukoma said to Jakove and me, "*Madoda*,[1] I miss my little girl. Let's go see the mother." And here we were, hearing them talk civilly. I hadn't made a single entry in my notebook, entranced by the smoothness of this meeting, the way it unfolded like an event willed by a superior power. Mai Lily laughed and tilted her neck as if she wanted Mukoma to kiss it; but she fluffed like a rooster when he mentioned a new arrangement for their daughter.

"You've no business asking about her," she said, moving out of what could be taken as intimate space. "Who do you think you are, standing here like you and I have something in common?"

_____

1   *madoda* - a Ndebele term/word for men.

I wanted to say, "You have something in common, which is why you are meeting," but I did not want to meddle in Mukoma's affairs.

"So you're finally telling me she is not my daughter?" Mukoma said, his voice shaking.

"You're the father, but that doesn't make her your daughter!" she shouted. "Get that into you thick skull!"

"That's a new one," Jakove whispered.

Mukoma tilted his head to show that he had not heard Mai Lily properly. Jakove and I moved closer and tilted our heads too. Anyone who saw us would have noticed three men paying attention to a woman who was about to say something damaging. But Mai Lily didn't drop the bomb yet; instead, she clicked her tongue in disgust and rested her hands on her waist like she was posing for a photo.

Mukoma glanced at us, but when he turned to her, he laughed and stepped closer, flirtatiously. He looked quite turned on, his arms extended, but she pushed him hard.

"What is this?" Mukoma said. "All I want to know is how she's doing."

"Why do you care?" she said. "Are you not happy with your new bitch anymore?" She pushed him again and said, "Get lost!" Then she started walking away, the stamp of her feet signalling the end of the meeting. Mukoma would not let her leave him standing there like an idiot. No one wanted that. Even Mai Lily had to have known this because, as she walked, the tilt of her shoulders seemed to say, "Stop me, if you can."

Mukoma pulled her roughly and looked at her face intently, but she shook herself free and hit him in the stomach with her elbow. He patted his beer stomach, cast a glance at us, stiffened, and then slapped her on the face, like in old times. He then held both her arms up and thrust himself forward as if he was going to kiss her, but Mai Lily leaned sideways and kicked him on the shin. He released her, looked at us again, and then sent a fist towards her face, which she dodged. She turned, dashed away but she swung back and, before Mukoma could throw another punch, she dropped to her knees like her legs had disappeared under her. Suddenly, her hands were glued to Mukoma's crotch and we heard the familiar whisper of an opening zipper. Jakove looked away and said, "Oh, oh, oh!", but I tugged his hand because I had just remembered Mai Lily's promise. I didn't know whether I should intervene. I looked at Jakove for guidance, but he was still facing away, only turning when Mukoma groaned as Mai Lily mumbled obscenities and assaulted Mukoma's crotch.

Mukoma twisted his waist and thrust his shaking legs backwards, but Mai Lily clung on. Why didn't he just push her head? He had hands that could form into fists to strike her, but he didn't use them. He bent forward instead, and kneed her on the chin. She disengaged with a scream, but suddenly gripped his left hand and stuck his index finger in her mouth; then closed her eyes and started chewing.

"*Mayebabo!*"[2] Mukoma cried, his voice registering extreme pain.

That's when Jakove and I jumped into action. I grabbed her collar from behind and pulled. Jakove hit her head with a fist and wrung his hand as if he had struck a rock. He then looked on the ground, but not finding what he wanted, removed his shoe and whacked her on the head with it. She did not relent. Jakove removed the other shoe and hit her with both, to no effect. I pulled and pulled; then I fell on my back under her mass, whose softness began to excite me. She slapped me hard across the face and shouted, "Stupid pervert!" The sting of the slaps was nothing compared to the force of her fist on my right eye. Mukoma and Jakove kicked her, and when they missed, they kicked me. They wrenched her off me and she fell on her back. But before they could touch her again, she sprang up, spat, and shouted, "Next time I bring a razor!" Then she sped away. I rose and was about to sprint after her, but Jakove stopped me. A few people had gathered, watching us and drawing closer. "*Sva-a!*"[3] Jakove shouted, and he shoed them away like birds.

---

2   *Mayebabo!* - a cry of pain

3   *sva-a* - go away! (used when jeering at someone who should be ashamed of his/ her deed.)

We focused our attention on Mukoma, who was groaning and cursing.

"Leave the finger alone!" he said to Jakove. "Check the main area. I can't feel a thing there!"

Jakove got to work, like a doctor, while I tore a piece of my shirt to tie around the finger, which was bleeding. When I touched it, Mukoma said, "Careful there; she will regret the day she was born."

Jakove looked up and said, "The goods are in order, comrade."

Mukoma started limping, but he soon stopped and bent in pain. "Are you sure there's no damage?" he said.

"She left you just a warning—a little cut, but that's all," Jakove said. "Can you feel anything though?" When Mukoma didn't answer, Jakove started laughing, but stopped immediately because no one else was laughing. "That woman has become a monster," he said.

"She is a hyena," I said, but Mukoma shot me a warning glance, and I closed my mouth. The way things looked, we had a long night ahead of us.

I could not help but think about how simple the beginning had been, when one Saturday afternoon Mukoma brought her home for the first time and said, "I present to you a new sister-in-law." A city woman, light-complexioned and voluptuous. He had met her at Kubatana Bar with the help of Jakove, who knew her from another bar. Their relationship had bloomed into marriage within two weeks. She said her uncle was a polygamist, so being a second wife did not bother her, as long as she stayed in the city while the other woman remained in the village. If Maiguru MaMoyo wanted to meet her, she would have to travel to the city for a stay not exceeding three days. She even told Mukoma that since Maiguru MaMoyo was barren and could not contribute to the growth of the Shumba family name, she could play her role in the fields. The new wife's terms worked for Mukoma, who just looked at me and said, "City women, I tell you, they are no good."

The two wives met after two months though. Maiguru MaMoyo arrived in Harare on a Sunday and told Mukoma that even though it was the middle of the harvesting season, she would not return home alone; the crops would have to wait. She said all that in her smiling way, telling the new wife she was happy that she had joined the family. In fact, she ululated in celebration when she noticed her junior's bulging belly. Meanwhile, Mukoma grinned while the junior wife rolled her eyes. I was there just observing how my brother was handling his business.

Later that afternoon, Mukoma walked to the grocery store with his new wife, leaving Maiguru MaMoyo with me because he said we had to catch up. What impressed me though was that he ran back into the house and planted a kiss on Maiguru MaMoyo's mouth.

Soon after they left, she pointed at the door and said, "So I see your works."

I didn't know how to answer, but I said, "Just trying our best."

I waited for her to laugh, but she averted her eyes to her sweaty palms, a twisted-lip expression on her face, the look she gave whenever Mukoma failed to come home on major holidays. Back then I had learned not to ask her what was wrong, but now we had to catch up, and the silence was becoming awkward, so I said, "How is the maize plot this year?" She did not even look at me. "The one with the two anthills," I added.

"Babamunini, just shut up, okay?" she said and looked away.

I had heard her, so I sank deeper into the sofa. When her shoulders started quivering, I grabbed a book, locked the door, and sat listening to her sobs. Even though she was talking and laughing again by the time they returned, I knew that the little party we had that evening did not mean a thing to her. It meant nothing to Mai Lily as well because within a week, the whole neighbourhood of 40th Crescent would crowd at the house, watching not a fight of fists, not a scratching and mauling-off of skirts and petticoats, but a contest of words, big boulders that the two wives threw at each other while I stood between them holding my chin and looking at the ground. When Mukoma arrived, the crowd disappeared, and that night the two women received their first lesson about living together well.

After the long talk, Mukoma asked me to come outside with him.

"How come you let them fight in public?" he asked as soon as the outside breeze greeted our faces.

"I didn't think they were fighting," I said. "They were just talking."

"Like that? Thinking: 'Ha, the wives of my brother are just talking.'" He raised his voice. "Like that?"

"They were not loud most of the time," I said.

Mukoma sighed and said, "You can't let them talk to each other the way they were. Distract them; put on some music or something." He paced about like he was getting angry, then he came to a halt, and started shaking his head in advance disapproval of my future indiscretions.

I told him I would do my best. Distract them, put on some music, do anything for them not to argue. We went back inside, where we found the women cooking together and talking like nothing had happened. Dinner was consumed amidst laughter that night.

The following morning the wives woke up early and did the house chores cheerfully; one swept the yard while the other cleaned the house, arranging furniture and polishing the floor. By the time I dressed for school, they had already finished and were laughing over hot, steaming cups of tea and thickly buttered slices of bread.

"Tomorrow I will show you how to make fat-cooks," said the senior wife.

"You don't say!" said the junior wife. "You know how to do all that?"

"*Zvomene.*[4] That I can do very well. Ask Babamunini here," said the senior.

"Sure Babamunini?" asked the junior.

"You will be converted, I tell you," I said.

---

4   *zvomene* - truly

I started greeting them, but Maiguru MaMoyo stopped me: "No, Little Husband, we greet you, not the other way round." She then looked at her companion and said, "*Mainini*,[5] shouldn't we be the ones greeting him first?"

"You greet him then," the junior wife said and dropped her eyes to her cup of tea.

A cloud of confusion occupied Maiguru MaMoyo's face; then the junior wife looked up and burst out laughing. She raised her hand for a mid-air clap with the senior wife's hand and said, "Look at him! He gets confused easily, this husband of ours."

After the clap, they continued laughing their fresh, morning-tea laughter. The greetings never really commenced, so I ate my breakfast in silence.

* * * * * * * * * * * * * * * *

"You seriously didn't see anything wrong down there?" Mukoma asked Jakove.

"*Nada*.[6] There isn't even blood." He paused and said, "Except, of course…"

"What?" said Mukoma.

"I already told you about the little tooth scratch. Other than that, I think you are okay, man," said Jakove, who started walking away. "Your daughter's mother is crazy."

"She will pay for this. You know me," Mukoma said. He started to limp along.

"Do you feel any pain still?" Jakove asked.

"Well, no," said Mukoma, trying to walk straight, but he suddenly stopped, bent, held his knee and listened.

"You are listening to the pain?" asked Jakove, but instead of answering, Mukoma simply straightened up and resumed walking.

---

5 *Mainini* - junior wife
6 *Nada* - a Portuguese expression for 'no'

When we reached a bright lamppost, Mukoma examined his finger. "This is killing me," he said, pointing at his finger with another finger of the same hand. The cloth around the finger was dark with blood.

"Fati can get a taxi for us," said Jakove, looking at me.

"You're not suggesting the hospital, are you?" asked Mukoma.

"There's no other way. Look at the blood."

"I can't have them ask me what happened. Giving reports and all that; that's silly."

"Just say it was a dog," Jakove said. "Right, Fati?"

"It was a dog. She's a dog."

Mukoma eyeballed me and said, "You don't call my women dogs, you understand?"

Jakove rushed to my rescue, "That's not the kind of nonsense we want to hear now. She's a rabid dog. The reason we should get you to the hospital now-now."

"So we stick to which story?" I said. "Dog or person?"

Mukoma shook his head and said, "It doesn't matter, stick to the dog story. I'll fix this *hure*[7] later."

We were going to take him to the Emergency Room. He got worried when Jakove said, "We don't know what she has, but we know she sunk her teeth in important places." After a pause, he said, "Fati and I will pay for the taxi."

"Whatever you do, gentlemen, do it fast," Mukoma said.

I jogged to Chimbi Shopping Centre to get a taxi. It was only five minutes away from where I left them. When I reached Five Avenue, I couldn't believe that Mukoma was struggling with the pain caused by a woman he had once tamed; it was as if the roles had finally switched, her stubborn attack was reminiscent of the marriage days when she had at first always fought back when he beat her.

Three weeks after Maiguru MaMoyo arrived from the village, we had a sleepless night when Mukoma beat Mai Lily along Five Avenue.

---

7   *hure* - a Shona derogative term for a prostitute

Mukoma had joked that motherhood would improve her better than the bars and nightclubs, and she asked him what he meant.

"Well, you didn't laugh as much when I met you, did you?" he said. The Shumba men bring smiles to their women." He winked at Maiguru MaMoyo.

"More like scowls," the junior wife said. "Or, shall I say old age? Look at her. She is younger than me but see how worn out she looks."

Maiguru MaMoyo sprang up and pointed at her with a shaking finger, saying, *"Pfambi munonetsa!"*[8] Then she clicked her tongue to show her disgust for prostitutes and sat down so suddenly I wondered why she had stood up in the first place.

"Shut up, you childless, rat-eating idiot!" said the junior wife, showing the mischievous grin of one who knew she had scored a point. She then widened her grin, cashing in on her accumulated points.

When Maiguru MaMoyo leaped towards her, she sprang up and welcomed her with ready fists. I jumped and planted myself between them, but Mukoma pointed at me with his beer bottle and said, "Sit down, buddy." When I hesitated, he pointed again and stood up. I removed myself from between his wives and they locked arms like cows locking horns.

When they saw their approaching husband, they disengaged and waited, as if each hoped the husband would take her side. Mukoma walked to Maiguru MaMoyo and slapped her, and she immediately returned to her seat. When he slapped the junior wife, she showed him a fist, and then she struggled with him. Mukoma slapped her again, and she covered her face with her hands and stopped resisting. Mukoma walked back to his seat, opened another beer, and belched with satisfaction.

Silence descended on the room. I resisted the urge to initiate dialogue. Perhaps the women would apologise to each other, and Mukoma would

---

8   *Pfambi munonetsa!* - Prostitutes, you are a problem!

remind them to work well together. But the junior wife stood up, made as if she was going to charge at Mukoma; then she turned, snatched her purse, and stormed out of the house. We looked at each other, and silently agreed to relax.

After a while, Mukoma told me to check if she was outside.

"You know she's outside," said Maiguru,[9] who surprised us by rushing outside herself, and when she came back, she looked worried. "You angered her," she said, looking at Mukoma. "Not good for someone that pregnant."

"*You* angered her!" Mukoma retorted, pointing at her with a shaking finger.

"We need to go after her," she said. "It's not right for her to be out there."

Mukoma wore his shoes, and told us to do the same.

Soon, we were outside, husband and wife exiting the fence through the front gate and I through the back. We converged on Five Avenue where we found her waving down a car. Fortunately, it did not stop. We ran and caught up with her, but she continued to march on as if she had not seen us.

"And now where do you think you're going?" Mukoma said, dashing in front of her to block her way. I expected him to slap her at this point; just a slap, nothing more, but he just raised his voice and said, "I'll lose my patience. You hear me!"

"Mainini, return home," Maiguru MaMoyo pleaded. "This can be talked over."

The junior wife ignored her. I opened my mouth to say something, but she gave me a dirty look. Then Mukoma grabbed her elbow and kicked her, a weak, warning kick. She staggered to the edge of the road, and then before she fell she swung around and struck Mukoma in the stomach with her fist.

---

9   Maiguru - elder brother's wife

"*Iyavozve!*[10] Are we fighting now?" shouted Maiguru MaMoyo.

"I'm going to kill her, watch this!" said Mukoma, who released a punch that she dodged.

Cars honked, but the two continued to struggle; weaving in and out of the middle of the road; then they slipped and fell on the grassy roadside. Down there, they rolled for a moment, but she got up first and started to run, smack in the middle of the road so that a few cars had to swerve around her. Mukoma sprang up and chased after her. He pulled her to the side of the road and they continued to struggle, ignoring our pleading.

If it were not for her pregnancy, I was certain Mukoma would have knocked her out already, but he was being careful in the way he kicked and punched. Yet when she hit him, she exerted herself. In some ways, it was fun to watch, only a bit embarrassing because we were in public view of the drivers zooming by.

"You know what, I have no time for this!" said Maiguru MaMoyo suddenly.

First, the two of us slowed down, and then we stopped altogether. I, too, was getting tired of this. We watched as they wrestled. He punched and she punched back. He swore and she swore right back. All this looked childish, and Maiguru MaMoyo's anger was unmistakable. By the time we reached Glen View 1, Mukoma looked exhausted, but the wife was marching on. At the first right intersection off Five Avenue, she turned left and Mukoma jumped to block her.

"What is this? Are you trying to have me damage you?" he asked.

It had become clear that she was going to Jakove's house.

"Is this some kind of game, where do you think you are going now?"

"None of your business!" she said, speeding up.

Shortly, we reached Jakove's house and, as if he had been expecting us, he ran out and told them to stop acting like fools. Although they

---

10   *Iyavozve!* - (It's an exclamation of surprise following someone's unexpected action)
        What's the matter!

continued to grumble and curse, they listened as Jakove lectured them on the importance of getting along.

"I didn't do things to make you come to this point," Jakove said.

"This is not the time for history," Mukoma said.

The wife tilted her head and said, addressing Jakove, "So this is what you told me was a man? What a waste of time!"

Jakove shook his head and said, "I did my job; the rest is up to you two."

"What are they talking about?" Maiguru MaMoyo asked me.

"I have no idea," I said. I knew, but Maiguru MaMoyo was not supposed to know these details.

The new wife stood up and, while pointing between Mukoma's legs, said, "I will chop it off one day." She then burst out laughing.

Mukoma was about to strike again, but Jakove and I restrained him. She marched off without turning.

"Let her go," Jakove said. "You know the anger of a pregnant woman; she will be fine."

Indeed, when we arrived home that night, she was sound asleep.

* * * * * * * * * * * * * * *

When I returned with the taxi, I jumped out to open room for Mukoma in the front seat, but Jakove said, "He has to sit in the back where there is more room. I will sit with him. You sit there and direct the driver."

"Gomo or Parirenyatwa?" I asked Mukoma.

"Gomo, of course. Dont' act like you haven't gone to Emergency," he said with a gruff voice.

The driver said, "Who is sick?"

"Just drive!" said Jakove, loudly. "That's not your business, right?"

"I also have to know why I am taking people to hospitals."

"And those people don't pay you to drive?" said Jakove.

"Not if they die on the way," said the driver.

"Just take us to Gomo, please," I said. "It's nothing big."

The Emergency Room was crowded, but what I didn't know was how long it would take Mukoma to be seen by a doctor. Jakove shook his head and said, "I don't see anyone being helped here."

Quite audibly, so that a few heads turned our way, Mukoma said, "The whore, I will kill her for this."

"The dog, remember?" Jakove said sleeply.

"Or the bitch," I said, with a low voice, but they ignored me.

After thirty minutes, Mukoma suggested to go home. Even as Jakove shook his head in objection, Mukoma added, "We will just worry about everything tomorrow."

"We're here, so we're here," Jakove said. "You're not going home in that condition."

"You are just being stubborn, Jakove," Mukoma said.

"I know, but still, we have to make sure you are seen tonight."

"Right," I said. "We don't know what she has. There is the danger of an infection."

Mukoma sighed in resignation.

The waiting was tortuous. I had not brought a book to read, except my notebook in which I could scribble things, but I was not in the mood to write. I dozed off, and when I woke up, the queue had still not moved.

Soon it would be time to go to work. Jakove suggested that we leave Mukoma there. We would come back after work, if needed.

On our way out of the hospital, I started thinking about what lie I would tell Mukoma's wife for our staying out late all night. When I asked Jakove, he said, "Think like a man. It was a dog." He paused. "If she insists on finding out more, come up with more lies. You are educated, man."

"I am educated enough to know that lying will not get us anywhere."

"But is this the first time you have lied for your brother?"

"Could it be possible that, perhaps, I'm tired of it?"

"You can be tired, but that does not mean that you should stop. We all lie."

I shook my head and focused my mind on how soon Mukoma would see his daughter, and how much time would elapse before Mai Tari kicked us out of her house.

Kennedy

The entrance to Kubatana Bar was crowded with peanut vendors and prostitutes. I shook my head as I tried to think about how the two groups worked in harmony. We entered the floodlit bar slowly. Mukoma and Jakove, the regulars here, walked in front of me, turning every now and then to check if I was still following them. I could not blame them; I didn't feel comfortable in beer halls, and this was the first time Mukoma and Jakove had ever asked me to come with them. They told me it was to celebrate my upcoming trip to the United States, but they hadn't specified how we were going to do that. I suspected, though, that a woman was involved. They wouldn't just bring me here to drink with them. It's not anything that I had ever done with them. Besides, if that's all they wanted me to do, we could easily have done it at home. So thinking that it was definitely about a woman, I started checking out the women in here, my heart skipping a beat each time my eyes caught the flesh of a half-naked woman, and there were many of them.

"Tonight, you'll see a side of me that will blow your mind away," said Mukoma, whose way of talking to me had gradually become more informal the closer my departure date drew.

"What your brother is saying is that he has something important to show you tonight," said Jakove, Mukoma's friend, whom I also called brother. "It's, as they say, a show-and-tell night."

I laughed in earnest and nodded vigorously. They were going to show me a woman, whom they would let me go with to some place…Perhaps they had booked a room for me at a nearby lodge, or, if there wasn't any of that fancy arrangement, then maybe the grassy space between Glen View 1 and 2.

The beer hall was packed. *Sungura*[1] music competed with the loudest of voices. Dancers on the floor slowed us. I wanted to dance too, to

---

1   *sungura* - a music beat that originated in Zimbabwe as a mixture of East, Central and South African sounds.

188

make this last night in the country even more memorable, to always remember Chimbetu belting tunes out of the loudspeakers, but the noise was too much for me to bear at first; I couldn't hear what the people were saying. Then there was the stench of beer and cigarette smoke blinding and suffocating me. Still, we threaded our way through the chaos, as shouting and staggering men waved at Mukoma and Jakove, who nodded at and thumbs-upped them. I was walking with celebrities. I was looking for a woman.

We reached a long table where Mako, the man whom Mukoma called *sekuru* because he had the same last name as our mother, sat with two prostitutes and another man. I lightened up and shuffled forward with anticipation. Although I fought hard to avert them, my eyes were on the prostitutes already. They wore bright-coloured dresses that didn't cover much of anything, as was to be expected, but the difference was that the younger one, perhaps twenty-one, caused a stir in my loins, which in turn caused my heartbeat to go faster. Her gaze had the familiarity of someone who had been expecting me. She could easily be mistaken for the girls who had been my classmates at college; because of her stylish braids, thick ropes that reached her shoulders, the slight touch of make-up, and the precision with which she had applied her lipstick. Then the complexion! She wasn't exactly light, but she wasn't dark either; yes, she had what I could easily call, in some fit of poetic rage, a caramelised tone. She maintained her gaze, and I noticed her smile spread across her whole face. She didn't seem drunk. If she was indeed the reason Mukoma and Jakove had called me here, they had made a perfect choice. I doubted that she was a prostitute; maybe she was in a situation like mine, of having been invited to the beer hall…yes, to meet me. I smiled at the silliness of the thought, yet wished that it could be the only truth.

Since my visa approval, when it had become certain that I was leaving the country, I had grown an appetite for prostitutes but, thus far, I had not managed to hook up with one. I had tried three times in Bindura clubs, but the whole idea of going to some strange woman's room had disgusted me; and I was also worried about running out of money before my trip. I had tried once in Masvingo, but the woman told me her last name and it turned out to be similar to mine; we both decided that sleeping together would be like committing incest. This one didn't even look like a prostitute. She was the kind of woman; I wouldn't dare approach if I had met her somewhere in town, classy-looking, cruelly beautiful. But the more she gazed at me, the more I became convinced that our destinies were somehow connected. I started to sweat. She seemed to know why I had been brought here. Typically, Mukoma and Jakove wouldn't discuss prostitutes with me, let alone bring me to one, but this was my last night in the country and the woman didn't even look like a prostitute.

She flashed a smile and, with a voice thicker than I had expected, said, "Sit here, honey!"

Yes, she knew. I moved forward.

"Leave him alone," said Mukoma. "He is beyond your league."

"Yes, way beyond," said Jakove, who turned to me and said, "Don't waste your time with these. Your future is waiting for you in America."

The way Jakove talked about my impending trip and about my waiting future, made me feel like I was already making great progress in life. As a recent literature graduate, I doubted that my brother, a self-trained electrician, would consider me successful, since I had not followed his advice in selecting my university major. Now, for him to say that I was above the woman's league showed that he respected me. Then to have the same sentiment expressed by Jakove was even better, but what woman had they brought me to meet then?

I needed a woman, any woman, before my trip.

She didn't look away, neither did I, even when a cloud of smoke from Mukoma's cigarette separated us. She was a woman, and that's what mattered. She even looked like Sibongile, the woman I had spent a long time pursuing without success. Well, maybe not, but still she

190

had a good smile, and she put it to use. She was perhaps beyond my league.

I wasn't going to pretend I was in love or anything. I knew, for instance, that she was a prostitute, which is why she was here in the first place, but I also knew that if the women who came here were considered prostitutes, which they were, the men they served, or who served them, were prostitutes too, which they were. I showed her the rare smile I always gave when I wanted to make an impression. Hopefully, seduction was written all over my face, or desire, which ever came first. She even seemed to be reciprocating the smile. There was something genuine about her smile, a smile of recognition, an affirmation that, perhaps, we were meant for each other, or that we had met somewhere before. *Don't waste your time with these,* echoed Jakove's words, but I wanted to waste a little time on her.

As I was about to take the offer to sit next to her, Mukoma showed me a different spot on the bench, and gave me a look that said this was not a negotiable matter; then he sat next to the lady and whispered something in her ear. She beamed and refocused her attention on her beer bottle. I sat next to Mako, who said something.

"Sorry...what?" I said, leaning closer to him.

"Your brother is going to honour you tonight?" he shouted, sending jets of spit to my face.

"So I hear," I said, accepting his extended hand for a belated greeting.

"Few men own up to..." He trailed off because Mukoma cast him a scalding glance.

"Gentlemen, talk about something else," Mukoma said. "Ask him about his trip." Then turning to the beauty, he said, "We can, you know, hook up later, after this thing I'm doing with my *mupfana*. Just make sure you stay fresh."

She said something inaudible, but it satisfied Mukoma, who turned to Mako and said, "So what are we drinking?"

"Well, you brought us the big fish here," Mako said, winking at me. "What does he have for us?"

"Ask him. He has a mouth of his own," said Mukoma, lighting a cigarette.

I took out my wallet and found two twenties lying close to five one-hundred US dollar bills. I got rid of the Zimbabwean currency by giving it to Mako who clapped in gratitude, "Well done, son of my sister. They surely don't call you Big Fish for nothing."

"Big fish?" Mukoma said. "Don't forget that I'm still the big fish, and will always be."

"Hey, don't mess things up for us now," said Mako. "He just gave me these to prove it." He waved the money in Mukoma's face. Mukoma waved him away and concentrated on the woman. She was still sending signals to me though, so maybe Mukoma was trying to stretch the surprise.

Jakove leaned towards to me and whispered, "How much did you give Mako?" But Mako heard him and showed him the bills.

"You can't empty your wallet on these drunkards," said Jakove, and to Mako he said, "Anyway, *sekuru*,[2] get us something with that money."

Several scuds of opaque beer were ordered. I was asked to join in the drinking, even after I indicated that I didn't drink. The men argued that with an important journey ahead of me, I had to loosen up and drink the people's beer.

"All right then," I said, "I will do it for you, gentlemen!" I received the pitcher from Mako and pulled hard at the beer.

The table clapped in admiration. No one here, not even Mukoma, had ever seen me drinking. So they were witnessing my first encounter with the beer pitcher. I drank some more, then the questions started coming.

---

2   *sekuru* - uncle

"So, about this journey of yours, what can you tell us?" asked a man I had seen only once, who was Jakove's workmate.

"Well, just a journey, travelling on vacation," I said, waiting for the brew to reach me again.

"Travelling all the way there for a vacation? Who does that?" asked the man, his face wrinkled with what looked like disappointment.

"Just a vacation trip, yeah," I said, receiving the pitcher from Jakove, and bringing it to my mouth in such a way that it blocked my view of the group. With my eyes on the frothy, opaque liquid, I pulled and pulled until I was almost out of breath.

Mukoma said, "Take it easy on that thing."

"Let him drink," said Mako.

"Let the man drink in peace," said the nameless man.

Jakove nodded in agreement. I drank some more, and Mukoma's face relaxed and he said, "I have told him to make money as soon as he gets there."

There was general consent around the table. Rapid nods and brightening eyes. Even the young woman nodded too, her face serious for the first time.

Mukoma continued, "Make money, make money, and make money. Do whatever work you find."

"Yeah, that's what this one…what's his name…? Robhi Mudamburi, you know my lodger Mudamburi?" said Mako. "He has been in South Africa for two months and already works, they say."

Mukoma shook his head. "We are talking about America here, *sekuru*."

"Sorry. America, that's right," said Mako, focusing on the beer mug.

Mukoma cleared his throat. "As I was saying, by the time he returns, he should be okay. We should all be rich by then."

"He will do well; he has an education," said Jakove.

"All young men should be like him," said the nameless man. "Men, real men, with dreams."

"But you're just visiting; that's all?" asked Mako.

"He can't just visit. He would upset the ancestors if he just visits and comes back empty-handed like Jabulani *wa*Mabhena."[2]

"You know that one is retarded; even Botswana couldn't stand him. But our man here, he's smart," said Jakove.

"He can always go to school when he gets there. I hear most of our young men make money bathing old women there." This was followed by general laughter, which I joined. Me, a teacher, bathing old what? I sat there looking at the progress of the beer mug from mouth to mouth, and at the young woman who was no longer paying me any attention.

"Why would he want to go to school again? He already has a degree, now it's time to be rich," Mukoma said, wiping the beer froth off his upper lips. He had passed the mug to Jakove, who practically buried his head in it.

"Young man, you better not waste that trip," said Mako. If you do, I personally will deal with you, straighten your head."

The other man whose name I still didn't know said, "Don't they say once you get there...?"

Mukoma cut in: "Okay now, enough about his trip. He is visiting... that's all you need to know for now. What's important today is what he is going to know."

"Yes, talking of knowing, why don't the three of us continue to our business so we can return on time, while the beer's still fresh?" Jakove said.

Mukoma whispered to the young woman, who pursed her lips and brought them to meet his. He fished out his wallet and pulled out a crisp bill, which he handed to her. She smiled, folded the money and inserted it in her bra. Lucky money, I thought, my eyes struggling to leave the cleavage alone. The woman looked at me and stuck out the tip of her tongue. I looked away and stood up to join Mukoma and Jakove.

---

3   Jabulani *wa*Mabhena - Jabulani of Mabhena

Outside was quieter as all the market women and other vendors were leaving. It was already after ten. I really needed to be in bed by eleven-thirty to get enough rest. This thing better be worth my time, I thought as we walked away from the beer hall. Mukoma led the way towards the older setion of Glen View, a place popularly known as the Weddings Section because when it was established in 1979, it had been intended for newly-wed couples. But when the country gained independence in 1980, the pursuit of equal opportunities for everyone brought a wave of house-seekers of all types. Yet the name had stuck; even those who were not married could say, happily, they had a house in the Weddings Section.

We walked past the terminus for city-bound buses, which was empty at this hour, except for a few homeless men who sat in clumps like anthills, past the emergency taxis rank, where several drivers were roasting corn. Business was slow at this time for them. We crossed the notorious 40th Avenue, which was known for muggings. The lighting was poor there, and this was where Mukoma had once beaten Mai Lucy, one of his ex-wives. The poor lighting had helped because the fight had not attracted a large crowd of spectators.

We walked down a moderately-lit street, going east. Some of the houses still had lights on, and in the few whose curtains were open, I could see people watching television or sitting in gesticulating groups. Looking through these windows, I was fascinated by the life in progress. On lucky days, one could see fighting people, maybe a couple or two, doing this or that. I always wondered why they did not think to close those curtains when they were doing these things. But some houses did not have curtains, which was even more interesting. Maybe we were walking to a house without curtains, where we would sit and be seen from outside by those walking by, doing whatever Mukoma and Jakove had in store for me.

What did they want to show me? Had they found a woman for me, so I would be one of those people who married immediately before departing to ensure that they would not marry abroad? These two knew I had no girlfriend and that I seemed not to show signs that I was interested in one. So, maybe, they were trying to fix me up with a woman. That had to be the reason - a woman for the departing man. Or, maybe, we were on our way to a *n'anga*, someone to give me good-luck charms and spiritual guidance before the journey. But if we were going to a *n'anga*, they could have told me so. Besides, I would have preferred one of those Apostolic or Zion prophets because they didn't demand animal sacrifices. But, this didn't seem like such a trip. It had to be a woman.

We exited the street and entered a dark alleyway. Now this was getting interesting.

"And we are not lost?" I asked, immediately wishing I hadn't asked, because I had sounded - well, funny, a bit drunk, or just out of place.

The two laughed and went further into the alley, as if what I had said was irrelevant, was not the point, was a spoiler of this surprise they had for me. This woman; she better be pretty. I walked faster and smiled at the prospect of cuddling with a woman in…what…ten, fifteen, twenty minutes? That would depend on how long the walk along the alleyway was going to be. We walked on, silent still.

After a while, Mukoma said, "Get ready."

"Do you think you are ready for this, sir?" asked Jakove, prodding me in the ribs with his fist.

"I just don't know what it is. So, I don't know," I said.

"Just toughen up," he said.

"I've to be tough?"

Mukoma slowed down, almost coming to a standstill. He turned and said, "After all the training I gave you, you tell me you are not tough?"

Before I was able to respond, Jakove chimed in, "Okay now, let's hurry up. Do you know what time it is?"

196

So we walked on in silence. The alley became wider and sufficiently lit and I noticed we were walking at the backs of houses. We were not going to steal anything, were we? Of course, why would the thought even get in my head? These weren't wartimes anymore, when I associated Mukoma with stealing things that belonged to white people. Sneaking in the darkness, headed for the Rest Camp near Takavarasha to steal the metal roofing sheets that he would use to make water buckets...

"Two more houses," said Mukoma. "Only two. I know you'll handle it. Don't you think he will, Jakove?"

"Would he be called a man if he couldn't?" Jakove said.

They were taking me to a woman. I felt a stir between my legs.

I had to say something to show I was still relaxed and flexible. The beer was taking effect too, loosening up those mouth muscles that often favoured to remain still in the presence of these two men. "What are you two up to?" I asked. "Because, if you ask me, this walking through the dark, emerging from behind the backs of houses, is getting creepy."

They both just laughed and continued walking. Calling them "you two" was usually not part of my vocabulary. But they had never played games with me before either; I was used to them thinking that doing certain things with me was inappropriate, considering that Mukoma was just like my father, being eighteen years my senior. He had told me many times never to follow his lead in matters of dealing with women. His first serious conversation with me about the issue was when he took a second wife, the one for the city. He had told me to focus on books and to worry about bringing prosperity into our family.

"That's your primary role in this family and, as you can see, mine is to make sure the family name grows," he had said. But I had finished at the university, a great achievement for our family. The fact that I was leaving the country for the United States was to him the first step to realise his dream of prosperity. So, of course, he would easily want to take me to a woman as a way to celebrate.

We negotiated our way through a tomato garden, which was damp. "Careful not to fall," whispered Jakove, who now led the way. We were behind a big house whose lights were off. We walked some more in the darkness, and then jumped over a short barbed-wire fence as we entered another compound.

"Here we are," announced Mukoma, signalling us to stop.

We stood in front of a shack, which had just suddenly appeared. Inside, light blinked. "Watch for your heads," said Mukoma, as he opened the door.

We crept into the shack where a woman sat, suckling a baby. There was nowhere to sit.

"Find somewhere you can fit yourselves," the woman said, voice relaxed, eyes looking at the baby.

"Sit, gentlemen," Mukoma said, as he crouched on a spot near the woman, whose legs stretched in front of her.

I found a clear spot between some dishes and sat. Jakove squatted near me. The woman torched me with her eyes, eyes so big and clear they seemed capable of swallowing an individual. I hope these men are not trying to fix me up with this woman, I thought, as I scanned the room, which had no bed. My eyes refocused on the baby and found their way to the full length of the woman's outstretched, smooth legs, all the way to the bare feet whose tiny toes seemed to wave at me.

"This is the surprise, young man," Mukoma said, pointing at the baby.

"Oh," I said. "The surprise?"

"Yes, he wanted to surprise you," Jakove said.

"He did?" I asked. But I realised I couldn't ask that question, so in the interest of toughness, I gave a brief laugh, and said, "Of course, he did."

I rose to a squat and edged closer to where Mukoma sat. A smile of approval worked its way across his face. "This is your responsibility," he said, still pointing at the baby, and the woman nodded and said, "What he is saying is..."

"No, Melu; let me handle this. I'm his brother."

"Fine then!" she said, eyes returning to my "responsibility."

"And what's that attitude, woman?"

"Attitude? You're the one with an attitude."

"Stop it, you two!" Jakove said.

Mukoma sighed. "Ok. Look, young man. I already told you about my problems with your sister-in-law, the one here in the city. As you know, when a woman starts acting up, a man does what..."

"No one wants to hear about that whore now!" the woman said.

"Why don't we just do what we came here for?" said Jakove, after which I shocked myself by saying, "Let's hear about this here." My finger pointed at the baby, whose little arms were flailing.

Mukoma licked his lips and crawled closer to the mother and her baby. "What we have here," he extended his arms to receive the baby who had been plucked off a stiff breast. "There we go," he said, patting the baby. "*Yesh, yesh*. How are you, *shir*?" He asked the baby, and looking at me, continued, "What we have here is the newest member of our family. He has no name yet, because we were waiting for you to name him, as long as you give the mother, your newest sister-in-law, something."

I pulled out my wallet. No Zimbabwean money was left in it, but I discovered that in addition to the five Benjamins, I also had a ten-dollar bill. I wouldn't have wanted to part with it, but the woman, blouse still unbuttoned, was waiting. "This is all I have," I said, handing her the bill. She held it against the light and, eyes widening, looked at me, at Mukoma, at Jakove, and then at the bill again, squinting. She buttoned her blouse and smiled, checking the money one more time.

"This is fine," she said. "Any amount is fine. This is actually very good." Then she got to her knees and started clapping, "Your brother was right about you. Thank you so much, our provider."

When the mother sat down again, Mukoma resumed, "Here is your brother's son. A man has got to do what a man has got to do, but I am getting old. I am showing him to you so you can always remember." He paused to watch my reaction, and satisfied by what he saw, continued, "I want you to remember, wherever you go, if you decide to stay in the US or continue to Canada, that you left a son here. Here is your son." He held out the baby to me.

I received the baby with steady arms. He was so light it didn't feel like there was a person in the wrapped thin blanket. As I was about to unwrap the cloth to verify the gender at least, my hand started shaking.

Jakove came to my rescue, "I wouldn't worry about trying to make sense of anything yet. Take it all in slowly. For now, just name your son and explanations will come later."

"Greet your son like a man!" said brother. "He is your blood."

"Hey you, little one! You, *shir!* I-I..."

The woman laughed. "This is all too new for you, huh? You forget you have some brother here?" She patted Mukoma's shoulders, who said, "Let him name his son."

I balanced the baby in the crook of my right arm and my skin crawled. He was so light and delicate I didn't feel like I was holding anything, but I held him carefully. Here was a new life, already with dubious beginning, but I felt his existence, as well as mine, was validated by this single contact. Perhaps this is what it felt to be a father holding a son.

Of course, he was not my son, but Mukoma, once he turned forty-two, had begun to tell me that the future of his children was in my hands. He had done his job of raising me, and I would take care of his children. Here in the city, he had a son and a daughter, aged seven and nine. In the rural areas, an ex-girlfriend of his had given him a daughter, who was now in Grade Two. And now this. Was he planning to take another wife?

"Name your son, young man!" said Jakove, and Mukoma nodded his agreement.

"Kennedy." I don't know where this came from, but it did it. This was my first time naming a baby. I repeated the name and looked at the baby as if to see if he realised I was calling him. He blinked his new baby blink, and started drooling. The men clapped rhythmically. The mother broke into ululation so suddenly that I was startled. I raised the baby to an upright position and right there, in the flash of a moment, I saw its vulnerability. I looked at him like I wanted to see a revelation. His stare was intense, as if his little dark eyes had seen me somewhere. The silence was broken by Mukoma. "Kennedy, it is. An American name, indeed."

"America!" shouted the mother.

I returned the baby to the mother, and for a moment my eyes locked into hers, and I realised we had not been formally introduced. Someone had to say something.

"Nice meeting you again," I said.

"Thank you very much father of my child. Thank you for coming to see us." She undid her blouse again and the baby clasped on. I averted my eyes and moved back.

"So, I think that's it then!" Mukoma spoke, stretching and yawning. "I will give him more information."

The woman clapped her hands and thanked me again.

We crept out of the shack into the darkness of the alleyway, walked silently until we reached the street. Jakove spoke first: "That was easy. Mother and baby liked you."

"I didn't know you would give that woman hard currency," Mukoma said. "You couldn't find regular money?" He paused, perhaps waiting for me to say something. I had nothing to say. So he continued, sounding more relaxed. "But everything went well, piece of cake."

"Did you take a good look at that baby? He looks just like you," Jakove said.

"I am surprised you didn't give him your name," Mukoma said, and my heart fluttered, as I remembered the baby's eyes.

"Kennedy is just fine," I said, as I walked faster.

Mukoma caught up with me. "I know you have questions. They will all be answered before you depart. For now, let's rush back to the bar and celebrate this."

I slowed down, but said nothing the rest of the way. As we reached Kubatana Bar, Mukoma whispered, "This doesn't get to Mai Tari at all, understand?" He waved at a woman leaving the bar, and then smiling, added, "But you can ask me any questions."

All I wanted was to enter the bar and drink myself into a coma.